TITLES IN THE SHADOW SERIES

THE PARTISANS

PIET PRINS

The Shadow Series 4

INHERITANCE PUBLICATIONS
NEERLANDIA, ALBERTA, CANADA

Canadian Cataloguing in Publication Data

Prins, Piet, 1909-1984
  The partisans
  (Shadow series ; 4)
  Translation of: *Vechters voor de Vrijheid.*

  ISBN 0-921100-07-8

  1. Wold War, 1939-1945 - Underground movements -
Netherlands - Juvenile fiction. 2. Netherlands - History - German
occupation, 1940-1945 - Juvenile fiction. I. Title. II. Series: Prins,
Piet, 1909- Shadow series ; 4
PT5866.P7V4213 1989   j839.3'13'64   C89-091151-7

First published in Dutch as *Holland onder het hakenkruis, III
Vechters voor de Vrijheid,* c. Jacob Dijkstra's Uitgeverij N.V.,
Groningen.

Translated by James C. van Oosterom.
Cover painting by Cornelia Van Dasselaar
Illustrations by Jaap Kramer

ISBN 0-921100-07-8

Printed in Canada by
Premier Printing Ltd. Winnipeg, MB

Table of Contents

CHAPTER ONE

BLANKERS RUNS A RISK

A week after getting shot during his fight with the traitor Poon, Kooiman had recovered well enough to get out of bed for a while. He was still weak on his feet, but it looked as if he would recover completely. That Monday Kris was sent back to school. He was still needed at home, but his parents didn't want him to get too far behind in his studies.

In the meantime, the refugees were being moved. Each day several of them left the hideout in the marsh with false identity papers and a destination elsewhere in the country. In the end, only Blankers and his carpenter colleagues were left. They had to tear down the barracks. If the Germans ever got wind of what had been going on here, no one involved would be safe.

This took them several days because they had to do the demolition work as noiselessly as possible. They spent the last night in the old shack that had once been used for duck hunting. The following day they brought much of the gear to another part of the marsh, very near the centre of the Wilds, and covered it all with several tarps. Usable supplies, like utensils and blankets, were brought back to the farmhouse.

Moving everything and policing the area took quite a while, but they managed to get it all done before evening. Then Blankers' colleagues left. They would try to slip to the city under the cover of darkness. They had been given an address where they could spend the night. The following day they would split up and travel to different destinations.

Blankers stayed behind on the island for about an hour or so to make sure all traces were gone. He buried some rubbish and spread armfuls of leaves over the telltale area where the barracks had been and then stood back and looked at his accomplishment with satisfaction. In the dusk, there was certainly no hint that anybody had ever lived here.

Pretty soon the wind and rain, and later the snow, would take care of the rest. Not even the most skilled and perceptive eye would find anything suspicious here.

*   *   *

It was time for Blankers to go, but he had mixed emotions about it. Despite the refugees' isolation, they had enjoyed their time together here. He had been able to see his son Jan quite often and his wife occasionally. Soon he would be sent far away; how long he would have to stay there before he could return to his village and family was a very big question.

"Come on," he admonished himself, "I shouldn't worry about that now!" Thousands of people were suffering much more than he was. He swung the shovel and the rake onto his shoulder and started down the path that wound through the marsh back to the open field.

It was completely dark when he finally came to the farmhouse. Everybody was glad to see him, and Mrs. Kooiman served him his supper—a plate full of mashed potatoes and a large chunk of bacon. Bacon was scarce during these tough times. Afterwards, she gave him a bowlful of buttermilk porridge.

Kooiman was up, his wounded leg resting on a chair. By now he was hobbling around a bit, but he still had to be very careful.

Kris and Jaap were sitting close to the stove roasting chestnuts in the fire. Suddenly Blankers was overcome by a longing to see his own wife and children; after all, they were so close—not more than a couple of kilometres away.

He had half-expected to be told tonight where he would be going next, but that wasn't the case. The previous afternoon, a member of the Resistance had dropped by to tell Blankers to sit tight. All the others had been taken care of, but they needed one more address. He expected that maybe they'd find something the next day.

That meant that the carpenter would have to stay at the farm for the next twenty-four hours. He suddenly had an idea; he hesitated briefly and then said, "It would be easy for me to make my way home in the dark.

8

If I take the fields and keep my eyes peeled, nobody will see me. During the day tomorrow I can hide out in the attic. It would be very strange if the Germans came back there again to look for me. In fact, it's safer there than it is here because the farmhouse is under suspicion and my place is not."

Deep down he knew very well that it wasn't a good idea and that he should forget about it. But his desire to see his family overruled his common sense.

Clearly worried, Kooiman shook his head. "I wouldn't do that! I understand that you want to go home, but it's safer here. If anything happens, it's much easier to get away from here. Remember, the marsh is only a hop, skip, and a jump away. You'd better stay here."

Mrs. Kooiman agreed with her husband, but Blankers had made up his mind. He promised to be especially careful on his twenty-four hour furlough. If necessary, Kris and Jaap could easily contact him at home.

The farmer and his wife finally gave up. They knew it was no good arguing. They understood very well the longings that possessed Blankers. And besides, the risks weren't really too great if he was careful.

Before long, Blankers was outside with Kooiman, who supported himself with a walking stick.

It was quiet; there was virtually no wind. The sky was clear, with a yellowish band across the western horizon.

They walked beside each other in silence until Blankers turned off to head across the fields toward the village. They halted for a moment as Kooiman gave Blankers a last word of caution: "Be very careful and keep your face down." Then he turned and hobbled back to the farmhouse.

Blankers hesitated briefly; all at once he felt that there was danger lurking out there. He could still go back. Should he?

His hesitation didn't last long. He shook himself vigorously, trying to get rid of that troubling feeling. Then he set out resolutely across the fields.

He was walking east. If nothing happened, he would be home within fifteen minutes. No, now that it was dark, it would take longer.

At the end of the field he stopped beside a bush and cut himself a sturdy branch. This was familiar territory; even in the dark he knew roughly where he was going, but he still had to be careful not to walk into a ditch. And all the while there was that nagging feeling, the feeling that there was something wrong.

*   *   *

Not far away a man named Jonas Krom was heading for the village. He'd had a good day; he had hunted right up until evening and had bagged three partridges, two hares and a pheasant. But he had wandered off further than he had thought; now he would be home later than planned. Once he had sold his catch he would have good cash to show for it! "Money makes the world go round." That was Krom's most cherished conviction, taught to him long ago by his parents.

His parents had long since died, and Jonas had inherited the dilapidated farmhouse with a few acres of weedy land. He was no good as a farmer. Besides, the only crop he cared about was quick cash. His whole life he had tried to make money in easy ways. He might have succeeded had he been endowed with better brains, but intelligence wasn't one of Jonas's strong points.

Stupid or not, he had a kind of sinister cunning about him and was never troubled by a guilty conscience. He had no conscience. Before the war he got into trouble with the law. After his first offence he received a suspended sentence, but the second time the judge had thrown the book at him. He spent a long time behind bars because of his crooked schemes.

Things were easier for him with the German occupation. During these times people like Jonas Krom could easily make a few bucks on the side. He wasn't a big operator; he made a small profit in the black market[1] and occasionally sold information to the Germans. He never

---

[1] The black market is a system for selling goods illegally.

10

joined the ranks of the N.S.B.[2], but he volunteered immediately for the German-run civilian police. Jonas loved to hunt, and as a policeman he was allowed to carry a shotgun--a privilege denied the rest of his countrymen.

Recently he had begun to ask himself how long it would last. He was convinced that the Germans were going to lose the war, and he was a bit worried about what would happen to him. But he hadn't had much time to worry about that today. Hunting had been excellent.

He was approaching the village now, but the farm where he and his wife lived--she was just as selfish and greedy as he--was right on the other end of town. Suddenly he tripped over something and fell headlong to the ground. Muttering and cursing under his breath, he began to scramble up again. But just then he spotted the shape of a person coming toward him. He couldn't see who it was, but he could see the figure moving against the background of the evening sky. Krom crouched low. Who was so foolish as to wander around after curfew? No one was allowed out except those with a special permit, like the civilian police, the members of the N.S.B., and a few people who worked night shift. But what would one of those people be doing out in the middle of a field?

The figure came closer. Huddling in the grass, Jonas could just see him. He had to find out who it was. There might be something in it for him. The Germans could be generous when it came to useful information.

Right behind him there were bushes, so Jonas crawled back to hide behind them. He wasn't about to show himself to whomever it was. He'd never been particularly heroic; he was better at tailing or spying on people than at confronting them face to face.

The minutes crawled by and Jonas was beginning to get cold. He was unable to see because of the slightly sloping terrain. And he was beginning to have his doubts. Suppose the guy had changed his direction. If so, he was just wasting his time.

---

[2] The N.S.B.--Nationaal Socialistische Beweging--was the Dutch Nazi Party.

Nobody came. "Tough," Jonas growled, disappointed. But just as he was about to straighten up, he heard footsteps coming toward him.

He went down flat on his stomach. He didn't want to risk being seen! It could well be one of those hotheads from the Resistance. Good thing that he had his gun with him.

The figure passed almost directly in front of him. Jonas couldn't quite make out the man's features, but for some reason or other, he seemed familiar. He had seen the man somewhere before, only he couldn't quite place him.

It wasn't a policeman; that was for sure. He obviously didn't want to be seen, and he even stood still occasionally to listen. That made Jonas more curious. It was beginning to look as if there might be money in it for him after all.

The man finally reached the path; Jonas lay flat in the grass, holding his breath and not moving a muscle. He didn't get up until his prey was about fifty metres ahead. Then he started to tail him. He made sure he stayed well behind. Once they got to the village, he would probably find out who the guy was and what he was doing in the middle of the night.

Twice more the figure halted and listened intently. It was just as if he suspected something, but both times Jonas quickly ducked down in the grass at the side of the path.

When he got to the outskirts of town, the man turned left onto a street. He quickly made his way to one of the houses.

*   *   *

Blankers had made it safely. It had taken him quite a bit longer than he had thought because the darkness had played tricks on his mind and had delayed him quite a bit. And there was something else too. Several times he sensed danger; especially during the last part of the trip, he'd had an uncomfortable feeling that he was being watched. He had scoffed at himself, telling himself it was only his imagination, but the alarm and anxiety continued.

It wasn't until he got close to the house that happiness and anticipation replaced his feelings of fear. He was walking home again,

12

home to see his loved ones. He hurried to the side door and tried to open it, but it was locked. He jiggled the latch up and down a couple of times and softly knocked.

No one was in a hurry to open up. These were strange times. Most normal people became afraid when they heard somebody at the door at night. It might be Germans about to carry out a search.

Blankers tried the latch a few more times until he finally heard somebody coming to the door. "Who's there?" That was Jan's voice.

"Open up! It's me, son!"

"Dad!" Jan yelled, quickly unlocking the door and swinging it open. Delighted, Jan charged at his dad and embraced him.

Still troubled by a strange foreboding, the carpenter quickly shut the door. Seconds later he was in the dining room, welcomed warmly by his wife and daughter Treesa. Both had such a stranglehold on him that it seemed they would never let him go.

"Hey, calm down, I'm not going anywhere!" Blankers laughed, but when he saw his daughter all choked up with emotion, something snapped inside him too.

Soon they were all sitting around the dining room table, with Blankers right beside his dear wife who couldn't take her eyes off him.

Oh, there was lots to talk about. Blankers explained why he had come—that before he was spirited far away he had wanted to spend one more night at home.

The smaller children were in bed already. Blankers and his wife took a small nightlight and went upstairs to check on them and kiss them goodnight. Of course they were fast asleep and didn't notice a thing.

It was home, and it was beautiful to be home. Mrs. Blankers had carefully saved up some real coffee and this was the time to have it. For the first time in years they enjoyed something they had always taken for granted before the war, and the real coffee made the occasion even more festive.

They talked about the children and their schools. They talked about the escapades of five-year-old Tonni, who was still home with his mother. They talked about hundreds of other things that would have seemed trivial to outsiders but were music to Blankers' ears. They also

14

talked about their worries and problems, of which Mrs. Blankers had more than her share.

Treesa and Jan were delighted to be part of an adult discussion. When Dad once again urged them to help Mom in as many things as possible they felt a twinge of shame. They had promised that before, many weeks ago, but they hadn't always kept their word. They were doubly ashamed because they knew that Mom was having a rough time.

All of them realized very painfully that this reunion wouldn't last long. This visit was a lull in the middle of the storm that could easily destroy their happiness forever.

Blankers would have to leave again tomorrow. It might be a long time before they would see each other again.

Maybe they never would see each other again here on earth. But that was the kind of depressing thought no one wanted to entertain just then. They were determined to enjoy this moment to the full. And who knew, deliverance might come soon! It had already come for the whole southern part of the Netherlands. And God could easily do for the rest of the country what He had done for the south.

It was getting late and Mrs. Blankers knew it. It was important for Treesa and Jan to get to bed soon.

"Hand me the Bible, Jan," said Mr. Blankers. Jan took the Bible down from its familiar place on the shelf. Blankers paged through it briefly and then read Psalm 91: "He that dwelleth in the secret place of the most High shall abide under the shadow of the Almighty."

The Bible reading over, Mr. Blankers prayed quietly and fervently. He prayed for protection for his loved ones, for mercy for all the oppressed, and for a speedy end to the war and release from the oppressor's yoke.

Then they kissed goodnight and went to bed.

CHAPTER TWO

IN THE HANDS OF THE ENEMY

The early hours of the morning were cold and dark. Another hour and the sun would rise. Already, far off in the east, the thick darkness was beginning to lighten.

A German armyvan roared down a village sidestreet, carrying a noncommissioned officer and three soldiers.

The streets were completely deserted, but behind their doors many people heard the roar of that engine. These days the sound of any engine frightened people awake. They lay shaking in bed, hoping desperately that the noise would go somewhere else.

It turned into another sidestreet and approached the outskirts of the village. Then it screeched to a halt in front of the Blankers' residence. The four occupants jumped out and quickly walked up to the house. The non-com posted two soldiers at points where they could keep an eye on every exit. Accompanied by the third soldier, he walked up to the front door and yanked hard on the doorbell.

Blankers and his wife were jolted awake at the same time. Horrified, they sat up and listened.

There it was again! Immediately it was followed by the loud crash of a fist on the door and a harsh command: *"Aufmachen! Schnell!"*[3]

"Germans! Hide, quick!" blurted Mrs. Blankers, terrified.

Her husband shook his head. "There's no place to hide in the house. They'd find me for sure. Somebody has betrayed me."

He got out of bed and walked to the front door, not bothering to dress. He motioned his wife to stay behind.

---

[3] Open up! Quickly!

A flood of emotions rushed through the carpenter, but he managed to compose himself. He opened the front door bravely and then stood there, very calmly, even when the non-com thrust the barrel of his luger into his face.

"Sind sie der Blankers?"[4] the non-com barked.

"Yes," Blankers replied calmly.

"Schnell fertig machen! Sie gehen sofort mit!"[5]

Blankers didn't try to resist. There was no way out of this. He was covered, and besides, there were probably more soldiers outside.

Followed by the two soldiers, he silently went back into the room to get dressed.

Jan, who slept upstairs, had awakened. He wondered drowsily what was going on. He was aware only of the sound of strange, menacing voices. But then suddenly it sank in that they were speaking German!

He leaped up, seized by a horrible fear.

"Dad," he moaned. "They're taking him away." Wildly he opened his bedroom door and scrambled down the staircase.

He saw his parents standing in the living room, his dad almost dressed. His mother, wrapped in a housecoat, stood by with tearful eyes and a package she wanted to give to her husband. There were also two German soldiers, the one armed with a rifle, the other with a·luger.

Jan knew what it all meant at once. He ran to his dad and threw his arms around his waist. Then he began to sob.

Blankers was having a hard time controlling himself; he ran his fingers through the boy's hair and tried to calm him down.

"Weiter machen!"[6] the non-com barked again. Blankers gently released the boy's arms and set him down on a chair. As he continued dressing, he tried to calm the boy down.

---

[4] Are you Blankers?

[5] Hurry up and get ready! You are going with us now!

[6] Keep going!

"We have to keep calm, Jan. This is the way the Lord wanted it. Let's hope He also wants me to come home again someday. God will take care of you. And don't forget about your promise, help Mom as much as you can."

Jan heard the voice but the words didn't seem to register. Still, his father's voice had a soothing effect on him as he tried to fight back his tears.

Blankers kissed his wife and son and said a few things in parting, all the while spurred on and bullied by the non-com, who thought Blankers was taking too much time.

"Say goodbye to the others and trust in God. He may bring me back sooner than we think. He knows what's good for us; we'll have to accept whatever He decides!"

His head held high, the carpenter walked out. Soldiers pushed him roughly into the back of the van. Two of them got in behind him, slammed the door shut, and drove off. In the faint dawn light, Jan and his mother saw the van disappear around the corner. Then they sat down in the living room, trying to absorb this horrifying shock. The tears started all over again when Treesa came down and was told what happened. When the little ones got up, they couldn't understand what was going on. Had Dad been taken away by the Germans? But he wasn't even here. All they really knew was that something was seriously wrong.

Mrs. Blankers busied herself with caring for the children to alleviate her grief and confusion. She sent the younger ones to school but allowed Treesa and Jan to stay home.

Jan was upset with God. Didn't God rule all things? Just last night his dad had prayed for the Lord's protection. He had read Psalm 91 about the shadow of the Almighty. And just hours later, his dad was taken away by those dirty Germans! They might even kill him! Why didn't the Lord protect him?

Outwardly gloomy and depressed, Jan sat for a long time staring into space. His mother suspected what was going on inside him. When the others were off to school, she sent Treesa and Tonni out on an errand.

At first Jan refused to talk, but then he blurted everything out. He couldn't understand why the Lord would do such a thing! God was the Almighty, wasn't He, and since his dad was a child of the Lord, why hadn't God protected him? Didn't the Bible say that God takes care of His children?

Mrs. Blankers just let him pour out his heart. Then she said very calmly but decidedly, "Still, you have to believe that God doesn't lie. Against His will not one hair can fall from our head. But sometimes it is necessary for us and for the coming of His kingdom that we suffer or even die. Think back to the time of the martyrs. Do you really think that the Lord left them to fend for themselves when they were sent to the stake? No, He remained so close to them that many of them died with a song on their lips! We know God will take care of us, even through death. That's true for Dad also.

Jan listened. Gradually, the storm within him began to die down.

True, he still couldn't understand all of it, not with his head at least, but he began to sense that the Lord's ways are higher than ours and that He always will remain our gracious Father, even when He severely tests His children.

Mrs. Blankers herself was comforted as she tried to explain things to Jan. Yes, she had a hard time accepting it also. She, too, was asking herself why it had to be this way. Her own heart rebelled. But as she was explaining the Lord's faithfulness to Jan, very simply, her own certainty in it returned.

Treesa and Tonni came home. Treesa helped her mother with the chores and Jan went to clean up the shed. After that he fetched his dad's tools and a piece of wood and made a little toy boat for his brother. Tonni was pleased by the attention his brother paid him. He laughed and chatted and appeared to have forgotten everything about his dad.

Silently, Jan scolded himself for having ignored Tonni and the other little ones too much during the past few months. He would do better.

Shortly after noon, the children returned from school. It seemed that a lot of the villagers already knew about Blankers' arrest. A couple of people had witnessed it. The teacher had asked about it. As a result, the little ones were even more bewildered and upset than they had been that morning. They asked Mom all kinds of questions but she said only that the Lord would take care of Dad.

During the lunch prayer, she implored God to grant relief from their present distress.

*   *   *

As it often happens in times of loss, the unhappy day dragged by. Toward evening Jan asked permission to go to the Kooiman farm. He said he wanted to ask Kris about a homework assignment, but that was really only an excuse.

Briefly his mother hesitated. Would it be wise to let him go to the Kooiman farm at this time? Maybe the Germans were still watching the Blankers' house. How much did the Germans know, and how much did they suspect?

20

On the other hand, she wanted desperately to know what their friends thought. She wanted to tell them what had happened and ask their advice. She couldn't go herself, however much she wanted to. She couldn't leave the children alone. For her to visit the farm might arouse suspicion.

It was quite normal for Jan to go. After all, Kris was his friend. The boys were almost inseparable. Was there any reason he shouldn't go?

She finally agreed. Jan took his books with him and promised to be very careful and return as quickly as possible.

He decided against going through the fields because it had rained the whole day. He walked through the neighbourhoods and out onto the open road. As he came closer to the farm, he noticed Gerrit Greven cycling up behind him.

Greven stopped and said, "I think your business is the same as mine. Hop on! I'm glad I caught up with you."

He didn't explain what he meant and Jan didn't ask. But from the tone of his voice, Jan concluded that Greven knew all about the arrest.

Jan sat on the bicycle carrier and Greven pumped along. They soon reached the farmhouse and rode into the yard.

The Kooimans and Jaap were sitting in the kitchen around a warm stove, but they all looked very depressed.

Jaap had come home from school at noon and told them all about the arrest. Kooiman had decided against contacting Mrs. Blankers. He was in a dreadful position. If Blankers had been betrayed, then it was almost certain that the Germans would also come to the farm. The whole day the Kooimans had stood watch, expecting the Germans to show up any minute. If they did, Kooiman would disappear into the Wilds. But the Germans hadn't come.

Now that evening had come and nothing had happened, they began to relax. But they were very happy that Jan had decided to come. Now at least they would find out some specific details.

Jan started in right away, fighting back tears as he talked about his dad being taken away by heavily armed Germans.

Kooiman wanted to know exactly what the Germans had said. Unfortunately, Jan remembered little.

"Where do you think they took him?" Mr. Kooiman asked.

Dejected, Jan shrugged his shoulders; he didn't know.

Gerrit then said, "I learned a thing or two. It wasn't until just before noon that I learned about the arrest. It really shocked me, I can tell you. It must have happened on the spur of the moment. Otherwise I would have seen it coming.

"I had to think of some excuse to visit the Ortskommandant.[7] Usually I go there only if I have something to sell them. They're all involved in the black market, from generals down to privates, because they can sell anything they can get hold of and make a profit. Anyway, that's my cover, unpleasant as it is. The Germans know I can deliver almost anything if they pay generously. They also know I won't play the informer. But they've got other people for that."

The dealer's last sentence was accompanied by a distinct note of bitterness in his voice. He halted briefly and then continued, "I quickly picked up some merchandise and took it down to the Ortskommandant's office.

"He was in a pretty good mood. He immediately bought a bottle of Schnapps, downed a couple glasses, and even offered me one.

"I didn't think his good cheer was very encouraging. So I started to inquire casually, but despite the alcohol, he wasn't prepared to talk. He only said he had caught himself a terrorist and that maybe now he would finally be promoted.

"I didn't like the sounds of that at all. So-called terrorists are usually. . ."

He didn't finish the sentence; he remembered that Jan was sitting there listening with bated breath.

"Anyway, a little while afterwards I had a private talk with my 'friend' in the office. He told me all about it. Blankers was indeed turned in."

"By whom?" Kooiman asked excitedly.

"By a third-rate stool pigeon, that good-for-nothing Jonas Krom!

---

[7] Commander of the city

He's always cozying up to the Germans. Whenever I run into him I have a little chat with him in a "friendly" way. The sneak considers me some kind of partner in this dirty business, I believe. Occasionally the Germans find something useful for him to do, but he's too stupid for big jobs.

"Last night he came to the Ortskommandant's office, all out of breath, and told him he had followed someone who had turned out to be Blankers.

"Jonas assured the Ortskommandant that Blankers was a dyed-in-the-wool Orange Bolshevik[8] and probably a very dangerous terrorist. He wanted to sensationalize the whole thing, of course, so that it would be worth his while."

"That scoundrel!" the farmer hissed angrily. The three boys looked at each other. If ever they got hold of Jonas Krom. . .!

"He would turn in his mother for a few dollars," confirmed Greven. "Well, last night he got his reward. The Ortskommandant agreed that it was an important discovery. He's smarting over his loss of Poons, just when he thought that he was going to make a breakthrough. But with Blankers' arrest, he might be able to pick up the pieces and make even more farreaching discoveries.

"So that's how it went. In the early morning a bunch of Wehrmacht soldiers were sent to Blankers' house to arrest him. They first took him to the Ortskommandant's mansion, where he was immediately interrogated. But Blankers wouldn't talk."

All at once, Jan's cheeks began to glow; however terrible the whole affair may be, he was immensely proud of his dad.

"Of course not!" he blurted. "He'll never talk!"

The dealer gave him a compassionate but sorrowful look.

"Yes, he's a very brave man, Jan. But don't underestimate the Germans! They've got methods to make anybody talk, even the toughest.

"In any case, when Blankers refused to talk, the Ortskommandant became furious. This morning he sent your dad to the city under heavy

---

[8] Nickname for those who remained loyal to the Dutch Queen from the House of Orange

guard. He personally got in touch with the Gestapo in the city. They've got a special detention centre there with professional interrogators, real bloodhounds, specialists in getting information out of people. They'll have to take it from there. The Ortskommandant assured them that Blankers had a lot of confidential information."

Gerrit fell silent; Mrs. Kooiman had begun to cry. Kooiman's tanned and weathered face had turned ashen, and horror registered in his eyes. He knew the dreadful torments Jan's father was facing.

The boys could hardly move. Jan became very discouraged. He would have cried out in his despair, but he couldn't open his mouth.

Kooiman was the first to break the silence. "Is there nothing we can do?" he asked.

Greven shrugged his shoulders. "I can't say just yet. Depends on the circumstances. In any case, I'll make inquiries in the city about where Blankers is being kept and whether there's a chance to spring him. If there's any chance at all, we have to take it. But I'll let you know the minute I find out. That could take a couple of days because I have to be very careful myself.

"As far as the farm is concerned, I don't think there is much danger just yet. The Ortskommandant still has his suspicions, because Blankers came from this direction, but he's not going to do anything until he gets a copy of the Gestapo report."

There wasn't much else to say or do. It was time for them to leave because curfew was drawing near.

Gerrit Greven stood up. "I'll be back soon. Jan, you'd better ride along with me again. That will save you walking most of the way. I'll drop you off just outside town because I think it's better we're not seen together."

When they left it was very quiet and very dark out. Jan had turned up the collar of his coat because the chilling wind was damp.

The bicycle headlamp was partly covered with black paper. There was a tiny hole in the middle of it letting through a narrow beam of light. That was a German "law." The whole country had to be blacked out to prevent English pilots from seeing where they were. It didn't make a whole lot of difference, but whoever didn't conform to the regulations was severely punished.

With only a little bit of light, Gerrit pedalled down the bumpy country road. He knew the road like the back of his hand, and although he sometimes couldn't avoid the potholes, he made pretty good time.

When they came near to town, Gerrit stopped and Jan got off. He thanked Gerrit for the ride and was about to walk off but the man called him back. He placed his hand on Jan's shoulder and said, "Keep a stiff upper lip, Jan. Maybe it'll be all right yet! As soon as possible I'll try to find out more. You can tell your mother that, but don't tell her everything I've told you tonight. That would upset her even more."

Jan nodded, realizing full well what the dealer was driving at. His dad had fallen into the hands of some of the worst criminals alive, and they were bound and determined to get information out of him. It was better for his mother not to know that.

"Thank you very much, Greven," he said, again choking back his tears.

Gerrit jumped back onto the seat and rode off. Jan walked on by himself, suddenly realizing that he had left his books on the farm. Well, it was too late to go back now. There was no way he could have gotten any homework done tonight anyway. Kris would probably bring his books along tomorrow. Besides, when his teachers learned that his dad had been picked up, well, what was a little homework?

Above Jan's head shone thousands of clear, twinkling stars. When he stopped to look at them, he suddenly felt less miserable. God was there. God could also see his father, shut away somewhere in some dark Gestapo cell. And what could even the Gestapo do against God?

From the heart of the boy a prayer went up to the God of life.

CHAPTER THREE

GREVEN BEHIND THE SCENES

Several days passed before Greven appeared. Jan, Treesa, and their mother all fervently hoped to hear something soon. The Kooimans were just as anxious. But for several days Gerrit Greven was nowhere to be found. It seemed he had vanished into thin air.

Actually, that wasn't strange. Gerrit needed information, and to get it, he had to be very careful. As long as he had no information he would not be apt to go to the farm. In fact, he might very well be in the city trying to set something up.

Jan was trying very hard to convince himself of this, and his mother agreed. But during very downcast moments, the boy doubted whether he would ever see his dad again. Greven's absence might mean he hadn't succeeded.

No doubt Dad was in the big stone prison near the edge of the city. Once Jan and Kris rode past it. There was a high brick wall around it with a heavy wooden door. The upper story of the prison could be seen from the street. All along the grey side walls were rows of small barred windows. His dad was probably behind one of those frosted glass windows, so close and yet so far away.

Another time they cycled past an impressive house near the centre of the city square. That was Gestapo headquarters, the home of the dreaded secret police, thugs who used unspeakable methods of torture to squeeze information from their victims. The shocking stories that were told about the Gestapo operations could make anybody feel sick.

Twice Jan had awakened screaming in the middle of the night, dreaming that his father was being tortured. At school Jan was withdrawn, unable to focus on his work. He had lost his appetite. Mrs.

Blankers forgot her own sorrow in her concern for her oldest boy—he had always been so close to his dad—and she tried to comfort and encourage him whenever possible.

One Tuesday afternoon after school, Kris and Jan got on their bicycles and started for home. Jan still had the same old contraption without tires. Kris still had tires on his wheels, but by now they were almost completely worn out.

There wasn't much going on in the city. After four years of war, occupation, pillaging, and persecution, most people had given up. There were hardly any cars, and most of the usable bicycles had been confiscated by the Germans.

There was also very little clothing; people had to stay inside to keep warm during these dark and sombre late autumn days. But even inside the homes, things were cold and cheerless. Whatever fuel was available had to be saved up for winter.

Unless it was absolutely necessary, why should people go outside? The stores were virtually empty, and what little was available was scandalously expensive and of poor quality besides. There was no reason for people to wander around in a depressed, forlorn city. Grey houses completely blacked out stared stonily into the streets.

Main Street was not entirely deserted. There was a two-wheeled cart drawn by a bony old nag. The cart was loaded with bags of war bread. It was greyish, sticky, and stringy, and no one knew for sure what it was made of. Yet it was still enough to make people's mouths water because they had to eat something. There were only a few pedestrians on the sidewalks.

As the boys rounded a corner, they almost ran into two pedestrians. One of them, to the boys' delight and surprise, was Gerrit Greven; the other man was a stranger.

The dealer took the boys aside and said to them in a muffled tone, "I'll come to the farm at seven-thirty tonight." Looking at Jan, he added, "You be there too." Then he turned and walked away.

Jan and Kris were stupefied. They wanted to run after him for details, but it was clear that Greven had wanted to avoid the danger of being seen. So the boys got back on their bikes and cycled off. All the way home they talked about what Greven might have meant by his message.

One thing was certain: Greven had learned something significant. But what could that be? Was it good news or bad? Well, they'd know tonight.

Jan told his mother as soon as he got home. She was at least as tense as Jan was and wanted to go with him to the Kooimans. But finally she decided that it would be too risky.

Jan was so nervous he could hardly eat. He left home long before seven o'clock. As usual, he took his books with him just in case he was stopped on the way. Then he could always say that he was going to a friend's house to do his homework.

On the farm, they had just finished supper. Mrs. Kooiman told Jan to sit down close to the stove because the boy looked worn out and almost frozen. She noticed that he had lost a lot of weight. He was taking his dad's imprisonment pretty hard. She gave him a boiled egg left over from supper. Despite his nervous stomach, that was a luxury Jan couldn't pass up!

Greven showed up at seven-thirty sharp. He apologized to Kris and Jan for his brusqueness that afternoon. "I couldn't talk with you any longer. It's more dangerous there than it is here. The less contact we have in the open the better it is—especially now that something is being planned for Jan's dad.

That made Jan sit up and listen. So there was a plan!

They all gathered around the dining room table, the three boys huddled close together. Mrs. Kooiman poured them all a glass of hot milk, which was a lot better than the usual imitation coffee or tea.

"Well, let's have it, man," said Kooiman. "Don't keep us in suspense!"

"I'll get right to the point," replied Greven. "I wanted to call on you earlier, but I had a lot of trouble gathering information, and it was even more difficult to work out a plan for springing Blankers."

"And did you succeed?" Kooiman interrupted impatiently.

The dealer shrugged his shoulders. "We'll have to wait and see. It's risky business. If it works, it won't be because of me but because of a

28

group of brave men back in the city. But anyway, we're not that far yet. Let me begin at the beginning.

"I contacted a couple of trustworthy souls in the city. At first, they were doubtful about the chance of liberating Blankers.

"You see, it's been done before; once they managed to free five political prisoners. And then, about two weeks later, a couple of Partisans managed to free a man by ambushing the car he was riding in from prison to Gestapo headquarters.

"Since that time, the Germans have taken extra precautions. Most of the prison personnel have been replaced with hard-core Nazi sympathizers—members of the N.S.B. and the Dutch S.S. They're all armed, and the prison itself has been reinforced. They built extra doors and iron gates to protect the doors. An assault on that fortress is out of the question.

"One of the men I contacted is the leader of a Partisan squad. He assured me that they would try to work something out. But he didn't think it was very responsible to sacrifice the lives of three or four Partisans for the benefit of one man."

Gerrit halted; the silence was painful, and Jan had to steel himself to fight back the tears.

Then the dealer went on. "The Resistance has one man inside the prison, a member of the N.S.B. who knows the Germans are losing the war and is now prepared to sell-out to save his own skin. He told us where Blankers is and that he's already been interrogated twice. But that doesn't help us very much."

"Isn't it possible to grab him as he's in transit from prison to Gestapo headquarters?" Kooiman asked. "That seems to be the only chance." They were all looking expectantly at Gerrit Greven.

He nodded. "That's what I thought too, but that didn't get us very far either. The procedure is this: if a prisoner is to be interrogated by the Gestapo, the Gestapo call the prison to make arrangements to have him picked up. They identify themselves with a particular password that changes every day. They say what time they're leaving and what time they'll be arriving at the prison to pick up the prisoner. Intercepting them would mean that a whole squad of Partisans would have to lie in wait, maybe for days on end, waiting for just such an opportunity. Of course, that's impossible. Besides, in addition to the driver, who is armed, there are always at least two S.S.ers armed with machine guns. No, violence is out. We'll have to try to fake it."

Immediately Jan's hopes rekindled. There was hope after all. Kooiman looked surprised. "How are you going to do that?"

"This is not my idea. It comes from the Partisans themselves. That's why I'm not going to tell you any details. Anyway, it boils down to this. We may be able to find out when Blankers is to be interrogated next. The Gestapo chief has an agenda listing the times of all the interrogations. He keeps that agenda in his desk drawer, which is always locked. But there are two people, cleaning ladies, who are in charge of cleaning Gestapo headquarters, and they always do their work at night. I know that one of them is for us, and she's prepared to help.

"Somehow or other the Resistance has managed to make a duplicate of the desk drawer key. The cleaning lady may get a chance to have a look at the agenda. She has to be careful about her colleague, who is not trustworthy. If it works, we'll know exactly when Blankers is to be picked up for interrogation, and then something will be set up that may succeed. If it works, I'll let you know right away."

That was all he would say, and Kooiman didn't want to know any more. The less he knew, the less he could betray if the Germans should get hold of him.

Jan went home, his heart racing. He knew there was no guarantee of success, but at least it was better than nothing. With God's help, his dad might yet be freed from those Gestapo beasts.

CHAPTER FOUR

AN INCREDIBLE DETOUR

FRIDAY, 9:00 A.M. Slowly and bitterly the city had earlier awakened to a grey, depressing dawn. Most of the canal streets were still deserted, but near the canal a group of city employees dressed in old coveralls were working on the brick surface of a street. It was near the bridge that crossed the canal.

Everybody was busy doing something. Some men removed the bricks while others dug a deep trench in the sand beneath them. Their work blocked all traffic across the bridge. It looked as if they were looking for a drain or a cable or something that had to be repaired.

Pedestrians could still use the bridge by walking across a couple of boards. they could also walk across with their bicycles, but nothing larger could get across. A man with a handdrawn cart complained loudly, but the workmen didn't pay much attention to him.

"You in that much of a hurry to go to jail? I wouldn't be so anxious if I were you!" joked one of the workmen.

The man got the message. Several hundred metres away on the other side of the canal, not quite visible from there, was the prison.

The workman's jesting didn't set well with the complainer. "Why didn't you put up a sign or something at the beginning of the street! Now I came all the way for nothing," he growled. When nobody answered his complaint, he snarled something and started back.

10:00 A.M. The chief of the local Gestapo was sitting behind his desk in the interrogation chamber. This was a room for those needing "special treatment," and he admitted only the most skilled of his assistants.

The chief had a round puffy face and hard, grey, pig-like eyes. In fact, in civilian life he had been a pig dealer. Since he had made it big in the Gestapo he never discussed his past anymore, but, behind his back of course, his subordinates often snickered that he was beginning to look more like his former merchandise. Needless to say, whenever he was in earshot they were religiously obedient to him because that's what Herr Muller demanded.

*   *   *

At ten o'clock sharp this powerful official of one of the most dreaded institutions in the world pulled open the drawer of his desk. He removed his agenda and paged through it. Then he nodded smugly. Actually he didn't need to consult the book at all because he knew what was coming. At 10:30 sharp the terrorist Blankers would be interrogated.

This would be the third time, and this time it would be do or die. Herr Muller was convinced that the stubborn Dutchman concealed a lot of information, and all he had to do was squeeze it out. He was bound and determined to make Blankers *ein Andenken auf lange Sicht*.[9] That was why the torture chamber for special treatment was being used.

*   *   *

Muller picked up the telephone and dialled. The doorman at the jail answered. Muller said the password and then, with a snarl informed the jailer that the *Haftling*[10] Blankers would be picked up at 10:15 sharp. The jailer replied that Blankers would be ready as ordered.

Herr Muller replaced the receiver and pushed a button on his desk. Seconds later, one of his subordinates came in, stood rigidly, and clicked his heels. "Heil Hitler!"

"Heil Hitler! Send a car with two armed guards to the prison. They're to report at 10:15 sharp to pick up Haftling Blankers. He is to be escorted to the special chamber."

The subordinate repeated the instructions, saluted, made an about

---

[9] something to be remembered

[10] prisoner

face, and marched off, deliberately thudding his polished boots on the hardwood floor. Herr Muller lit a cigarette and leaned back comfortably in his chair. He wanted a few minutes of meditation to prepare for this special treatment he would give to Blankers. A relaxing, reflective preparation was half the job.

10:07 A.M. The iron gate to the inner courtyard behind Gestapo headquarters swung open. A German military car with a driver and two armed guards drove slowly out into the street. Then the engine revved, and the car shot off toward the canal. It turned into a long street that terminated at the bridge across the canal.

The driver was in no hurry; he had eight minutes to get to the jail— lots of time. Near the canal the street veered off to the right. As the driver came around the curve, his plan was ruined. He cursed. Near the bridge the surface of the street had been broken up. The bricks had been neatly stacked up, preventing access to the bridge. Workmen were up to their waists in a deep trench.

The brakes screeched as the car came to a halt. The three Germans leapt out and started to rage at the innocent workmen in the trench.

The workmen looked startled but didn't understand German. They could figure out the general message. One of them, an older man, probably the foreman, shrugged his shoulders and said in Dutch, "Closed to traffic."

Well, that was already apparent to the Germans, and they were furious at the delay and especially at the fact that there hadn't been a sign at the beginning of the street warning them that the bridge was closed. But their raving and ranting didn't help a bit. There was only one thing they could do—drive back and take the next bridge, about half a kilometre away.

Their faces still twisted with rage, the Gestapo men jumped back into the car and slammed the door. They had to turn the car around, and there wasn't much room. Apparently feeling a little embarrassed, a couple of the workmen politely volunteered to help turn the car around. One stood in front of the car and motioned to the driver that he had lots of room to back up. Another stood behind the car to make sure it didn't back into the trench.

The back wheels went up onto the sidewalk; the car needed to go back only about a metre more before it could turn around. What the driver couldn't see was that there were a couple of boards lying on the sidewalk, one of which had three ugly-looking nails sticking through it.

"Just a little more!" shouted the man stationed behind the car. Anxious to help, he walked forward a little bit, but his foot kicked against the board and the board shot forward just as the car was inching its way back. And sure enough, the left rear wheel drove directly onto the board, right over the nails.

The driver shifted into low gear and the car slowly pulled ahead. The workman then saw what had happened and quickly lunged forward to pull the board loose from the tire, in vain.

The driver stepped on the gas and roared off the way he had come, shifting gears quickly to make up for lost time. The workmen stared after it dumbly. Then they briefly looked at each other and went back to work.

*   *   *

The driver was now in a hurry; in five seconds he had reached the end of the street. He blared the horn and turned left.

Then he noticed it. Something was wrong with one of the tires! He braked and jumped outside. The left rear tire had gone completely flat.

This second disaster made their blood boil. With no Dutch people around to yell at, the Germans began to shout and curse at each other. The armed guards blamed the driver, of course. The driver protested loudly and blamed the two guards. But before long, he realized he'd better get the tire changed. He opened the trunk, removed the jack and the spare tire, jacked the car up, loosened the nuts, and removed the wheel. Expertly he slipped the spare wheel on and chucked everything back into the trunk.

The man had obviously done this before, and the two guards helped him, so it was quick work. Nevertheless, they had lost precious minutes. It would make them late for their appointment at the jail.

10:12 A.M. Blankers had been fetched from his cell and deposited in a narrow hallway near the jail entrance. He was pale with fear. The news that he would be picked up had been crushing. It could only mean that he would be interrogated again.

He'd been through this twice already. The second time had been far worse than the first, and at the conclusion they had cold-bloodedly informed him that the worst was yet to come.

Blankers was terrified. Would he be able to keep his mouth shut during the pain that was in store for him? If he died, that would be bad, but it would be worse still if he were to succumb to their physical and mental abuse and blurt out all kinds of things that the Germans weren't supposed to know.

Maybe he didn't know as many secrets as the Gestapo hoped, but he knew quite a few. He was determined to keep his mouth shut, but he

35

knew all about the ruthless Nazi methods. He had spent the last few minutes in prayer, asking God to give him the strength not to betray anyone.

Prayer had restored to him a measure of peace. He tried to buck up and plan a course of action–something to focus on that might prevent him from giving in.

Then he heard the car. It stopped in front. Next came the loud clanging of a bell. This was it. White-faced, but suddenly very calm and resolute, Blankers got up.

10:15 A.M. The car Blankers had heard stopped in front of the prison door. One of the three soldiers in it got out and rang the bell. A small trapdoor opened. When the guard saw the German uniform on the other side of the door, he opened it and then unlocked the iron gate. He was taking his time about it, much to the chagrin of the impatient Gestapo man.

"Schnell, wir haben Eile!"[11] he barked impatiently. The guard mumbled something under his breath but knew he'd better get a move on.

With the gate and door open, the car roared into the inner court and halted in front of the prison's administration building. The guard inside the building had already seen what was going on. He quickly opened the door and escorted the two heavily armed Gestapo men inside. The driver stayed out to turn the car around.

They didn't waste any words. The German merely mentioned Blankers' name, and the guard hastened to fetch the prisoner from the corridor.

Head held high, the carpenter walked to the Gestapo men. At least he was no longer consumed by fear; God had given him the courage to face this ordeal.

One of the Gestapo men pulled out a pair of handcuffs and closed them around Blankers' wrists. The prison guard looked somewhat surprised at this precaution, but the other German assured him, *"Der*

---

[11] Quick, we're in a hurry!

Blankers ist ein gefahrlicher Terrorist!"[12] He added that they had been delayed at the bridge and had to make a detour.

The German pushed Blankers roughly and told him to get going. His cohort aimed his pistol at the back of the terrorist's head. The prison guard quickly opened the door, and the two Germans escorted their prisoner outside. They pushed and shoved him roughly toward the car. One of the Germans shouted at the guard standing at the main gate, *"Tor aufmachen, Schnell!"* [13]

The doors were slammed shut and the driver took off. Tires squealing, the car barrelled off toward the gate. It roared through and immediately turned to the right instead of to the left, which was the direction of the city. The guard, staring after the car, didn't give it a second thought. The bridge was closed, that's why they went to the right. He shut the gate again in boredom and no longer thought about the unfortunate man who was surely heading for the most horrible torture imaginable.

10:30 A.M. Inside the prison guard's office, a telephone rang. When the guard picked up the receiver he immediately recognized the furious voice of Herr Muller. The chief of the Gestapo was demanding to know what had happened to the *Haftling* Blankers!

The guard assured him that Blankers had already been picked up but that the car had been delayed because the bridge was closed, necessitating a detour.

The minute he replaced the receiver, it began to occur to him that something was wrong. Despite the delay of the detour, the car had arrived right on time; now, fifteen minutes later, it still hadn't gotten back to Gestapo headquarters. Ah well, that wasn't his business. He wasn't responsible for what they did. He didn't want to get involved.

10:35 A.M. For five minutes nothing had happened at the prison.

---

[12] Blankers is a dangerous terrorist!

[13] Open the gate and be quick about it!

Suddenly another German car came roaring up to the front gate and squealed to a halt.

Again two uniformed Germans jumped out. They were even more excited and more hurried than the previous pair. Angrily they shouted at the sluggish guard to get a move on. The guard was flabbergasted. Two visits from the Gestapo within twenty minutes. What was this all about?

The guard in the administration building was even more dumbfounded. He hadn't been informed that a second prisoner would be picked up, so he reasoned that these men must be delivering somebody. To his great dismay, however, they barked that they had come to pick up Blankers. The guard just gaped at them. Then his confusion made way for suspicion. Something was wrong here! The prisoner was supposed to have been picked up at 10:15 sharp, and that's precisely what had happened!

Now it was well past 10:30. It was strange that these men would show up now. On the other hand, how could he explain that urgent telephone call from Herr Muller? That had been only about five minutes ago, and Blankers hadn't arrived yet at Gestapo headquarters.

He couldn't figure it out, but he had a sinking feeling that something dreadful was about to happen to him. He invited the Germans in without explaining that Blankers had already been picked up. They'd have to wait, despite all their furious badgering. He quickly left to consult with his supervisor.

Minutes later he came back, accompanied not by Blankers but by the warden. He had given the warden a quick rundown of what had happened.

What followed was a strange and confusing conversation. It didn't take long for the warden to find out that these were genuine Germans, Gestapo people no less. They were beside themselves with rage when they discovered that the prisoner had been picked up already.

Needless to say, the unfortunate guard who didn't have an explanation for anything bore the brunt of their wrath. He was blamed for and threatened with everything. Even the warden turned on him, and the Gestapo assured him that he was heading for a concentration camp or for a firing squad because he had allowed the terrorist to escape!

38

However, the poor guard felt slightly relieved minutes later when the two Gestapo men were similarly abused and browbeaten by their chief, Herr Muller, on the telephone.

When he had calmed down somewhat, Herr Muller ordered them to follow the other car immediately. He would alert the local police. Blankers and the pseudo-Germans had to be caught, whatever the cost!

One of two husky Gestapo bullies, standing rigidly at attention and looking very much like a guilty schoolboy, replied timidly that they would execute Herr Mullers' orders immediately. After hanging up, they started to tear into the poor prison guard again. He had to give them an exact description of the car and of the occupants. The guard at the gate was also called in for consultation.

Neither man was able to come up with more than a vague description. When one of them remembered that the fake Germans had also talked about the detour something began to dawn on one of the Germans. Of course! They had been taken too! Those workmen had been part of it!

"Schweinerei!"[14] he roared and then ran outside, followed closely by his colleague. The flabbergasted driver, who still hadn't suspected anything, was told to drive to the bridge as fast as he could. All the workmen had to be arrested.

Away they went. The two Germans checked their machine guns and got ready to swing into action. But when they got to the bridge they saw only piles and piles of sand and a few stacks of bricks. There wasn't a soul to be seen. Not one person could tell them where the workmen had gone. . .

---

[14] Pigs!

CHAPTER FIVE

A HIGH TOWER

Blankers was prepared for the worst as the Gestapo men pushed him into the car. One of the armed guards was sitting beside him on the back seat. The other had joined the driver up front.

He was surprised to notice that the car headed away from the city. Then he recalled having heard something about a closed bridge. That must be the reason. They were probably heading for the next bridge across the canal.

But that wasn't the case either. Shortly after they had left the outskirts of the city, the driver turned onto a sideroad. They headed for some dark woods on the horizon.

The carpenter was suddenly seized by cold, paralysing terror. He'd heard about this sort of thing; the Germans would take their victims to some isolated spot in the woods, force them to dig their own graves, and shoot them down in cold blood. Was this what awaited him?

The engine roared. The car was going almost eighty as it careened down the narrow, deserted country road. All of a sudden, the guard sitting beside Blankers began to talk. To Blankers' amazement and confusion, the man spoke perfectly good Dutch. But what he said was even more astonishing.

"You can relax now, Blankers. We're not Germans, but fellow countrymen. Show me your hands and I'll take off those little trinkets. That was only to make it look realistic."

Blankers' mouth dropped; he couldn't believe his ears and was too flabbergasted to hold out his hands. This was just too much. This was incredible! But the chap took some keys out of his pockets and leaned forward to remove the handcuffs.

"Do you believe me now?" he asked, chuckling.

Yes, something was beginning to dawn on the carpenter. Was he free and in the company of friends? But he was still confused and choked with emotion. His next impulse was to jump out and shout and dance from relief, but his whole body, including his voice, was very weak. With difficulty he stuttered, "Thanks. . . thanks very much!"

"Don't mention it. It's all for a good cause. But we're not out of the woods yet. Those bloodhounds are probably after us right now!"

For the hundredth time, the "guard" beside him stole an anxious glance through the rear window. But there was nothing to be seen yet, and that was encouraging.

Ten minutes later they reached the edge of the forest. The country road became a trail through the woods that was just wide enough for the car.

About two hundred metres into the woods, the car pulled up in front of an isolated house, probably belonging to a game warden. The driver honked the horn and a friendly looking elderly lady came out through the front door.

"You'd better stay here, Blankers; we'll be right back," said the "guard."

The three make-believe Germans got out, leaving Blankers to think by himself. It wasn't until now that he began to realize the extent of his good fortune. Fervently and quietly he thanked God for his deliverance.

Presently the driver returned wearing civilian clothes. He quickly removed the German licence plates and replaced them with a Dutch registration.

Shortly afterwards, the other two also returned wearing civilian clothes. In addition, one of the men had been supplied with spectacles and the other had miraculously grown a mustache. They didn't look at all like the Germans who had pulled off the caper back at the prison. Both of them had bicycles.

They walked to the car to shake Blankers' hand and wished him the best. It was too risky to stay together because the Germans and their accomplices in the Dutch police would undoubtedly be on the lookout for a car with four occupants. The two men would cycle off in different directions and eventually return to the city. The driver would take Blankers to a new hideout.

Gradually, the carpenter sorted it all out. He once again thanked his liberators, but they shrugged off his compliments. The two men jumped onto their bicycles and rode off to find separate ways back to the city. It was better not to be seen together.

The driver had finished preparing the car. He chucked his tools into the trunk and went back into the game warden's cottage to wash his hands. When he came back, he said to Blankers, "All right, out you go. I've got another spot for you."

Blankers got out. His driver leaned inside, fiddled around with the back seat, and folded it forward. There was just enough room behind it for a man to lie down.

The driver grinned when he spotted the look in Blankers' eyes. "We customized the car a bit," he explained with a chuckle. "That's very useful. Well, get in, and I'll replace the back seat. You'll have to lie in a crouched position; there isn't all that much room, but you'll manage. At least others have."

"Is that really necessary?" Blankers asked hesitantly.

"You had better believe me! I'm sure your description has already been radioed out. There's every chance that we'll be stopped. I've got all the proper papers, but you have to be invisible."

Blankers needed no more convincing. He squeezed himself into the space behind the back seat. The back seat was then returned to its proper position, and the driver slid in behind the steering wheel.

It didn't take Blankers long to find out that his hiding place was far from ideal. Although there was no danger of suffocating, he felt cramped. The rough road with its potholes jolted his bones. He hoped he wouldn't have to put up with this for too long. He had no idea where he was being taken.

The driver finally emerged on the other side of the woods and headed for a paved road. After a few more zigs and zags down country roads, he reached a highway that led to another city.
Everything had gone well so far; the driver began to relax. They were almost there.

Just as he reached the outskirts of the city, he spotted a Dutch policeman and three German privates at an intersection. The policeman held up his hand, ordering the car to stop. Soldiers held their pistols ready.

The driver halted and rolled down the window. One of the Germans checked the exterior of the car and compared it with the information he had been given about the German car that had been used in the raid on the prison. It had Dutch licence plates, but the make was the same.

The policeman growled that he wanted to see the driver's papers. So he got them: a driver's license, registration and identity card, and a lot of other official-looking documents. One of them identified the driver as Willem de Jong, Regional Director of Food Administration.

The policeman was pretty well convinced that there was nothing suspicious. He took a quick glance around inside the car but didn't see anything. Besides, this man's description didn't fit the one he'd been given of Blankers nor of any of the three men who had picked Blankers up.

Just to be sure, he asked "de Jong" where he came from and where he was headed. The whole exchange was rather pleasant. The driver said he was on official business for the government's administration branch.

Blankers, of course, could overhear everything that was being said. Cooped up in the confined space, he died a thousand deaths. Apparently everything was all right, and the driver's papers were in order. Then Blankers developed a problem: an itchy throat and an almost uncontrollable coughing fit. He kept swallowing hard and biting down on his handkerchief.

Fortunately, just then the driver was finally waved on and drove off. Seconds later, Blankers burst loose with a loud coughing fit that just a moment earlier would have done him in.

* * *

Soon the car slowed down again. The driver wheeled into a narrow alleyway between two tall nineteenth-century warehouses. At the end of the alley was a large iron door. The driver beeped a prearranged signal on his horn and almost immediately the door opened. The car drove through and then came to a stop. The driver yanked the rear seat forward and invited Blankers to come out and stretch his legs.

The carpenter blinked a couple of times, surprised. They were inside a cavernous, half-dark, half-empty space, something that must have been a warehouse at one time. He spotted a few dozen barrels stacked up alongside one of the walls.

The driver laughed softly at the surprised look on Blankers' face. "This used to be a warehouse for wines and fruit juices," he explained. "There isn't much demand for it these days, but now we can use the warehouse for our own purpose. Please follow me."

They threaded their way among the barrels to a corner of the building where they came to a staircase that led to a second story. There were more barrels and drums there.

A second set of stairs led to a large attic. Toward the rear, a couple of rooms had been partitioned off. The driver opened the door to one of them and walked inside. It was quite a cosy room, modestly furnished. There were two elderly people there, a man and a woman. They didn't appear at all surprised to see the visitors.

44

"Let me introduce Mr. and Mrs. Gerritsen, who prefer to be called Oom Koos and Tante Miep by their friends," explained the driver. "And this is Blankers. Please take good care of him for now, Tante Miep!"

"Of course! He won't have any complaints," replied the elderly lady cheerfully. Her hair was already snow white, but her cheeks were ruddy and her eyes keen. She quickly pulled a couple of chairs up to the stove in the corner of the room. As Tante Miep poured the visitors a cup of imitation tea, Oom Koos inquired about the details of the rescue. Obviously he had been filled in beforehand.

Blankers just listened; he still hadn't gotten over his miraculous escape.

When the driver explained how he had talked himself through one of the police roadblocks, Blankers added, "I'm very much indebted to you, Mr. de Jong. It was touch and go, especially since I had to choke back a coughing spell."

"Good thing I didn't know that," replied the other, laughing. "Something else—my name is not de Jong. I had to use that name because that's what happened to be on the papers. Just call me Cor. That's the name I use in the Resistance."

Blankers quickly felt at ease. The elderly couple made him feel welcome. Cor went on to discuss a number of other things with Oom Koos. It seemed that the old warehouse had a lot of nooks and crannies that were used by the Resistance to hide refugees and that the elderly Gerritsens were responsible for all of them.

After a while Oom Koos said, "Now I'm going to show our guest around. Come on, Blankers; I'll show you where you sleep."

He opened a door in one of the side walls and they walked into a small attic bedroom, complete with basin, a chair, and a single bed. It was all very simple, but it looked and smelled clean.

"This is yours for the time being. Now I want to show you one more thing that may come in handy. As far as we know right now, you'll be safe here. But sooner or later the Germans may get wind of us, and then they'll probably come in the early morning hours, when everybody's asleep."

Blankers nodded knowingly. "Yes, I found out," he said ruefully, recalling when his house was raided.

"Excellent! Experience is a good teacher. Now then, the bedroom door has a bolt on the inside. Look, here it is. Don't forget to use it at all times."

"Will do," replied Blankers, "but I don't think that's going to stop the Germans."

"No need to. A few seconds—that's all we need. Here, I'll show you."

He walked to the opposite wall and opened a large clothes closet. There were a few dresses and coats inside. Oom Koos slid them aside and then reached for the wall.

"Pay attention now. There's a bolt down here. Look, I'm going to unlock that now. There's a second bolt right here, see? There, now that's unlocked too." He pushed against the little door and opened it to the outside. The space was big enough for a man to squirm through. Beyond the open door was the rooftop of an adjacent house.

"This is how you'll escape if you'll ever need to. I'll tell you exactly how to do that. Make sure you remember it; your life could depend on it."

Blankers needed no convincing; he listened attentively.

"In case of a raid, you'll slip out through here. Close the door behind you. There's also a bolt on the outside that you'll have to lock.

"Now then, right below this door is a ledge for the eaves. It's sturdy enough to hold you. Once you're out, you go to the right till you come to that corner. From there you cross over to the next ledge. It's not all that dangerous if you keep your eyes peeled.

"When you come to the end of the second ledge you'll see a warehouse with a flat roof and next to that another one. Between those two flat roofs is an open space of about two metres that is bridged with a thick board. When you come to the end of the second roof, there's a fire escape going down. Once you're down, you'll find yourself in an alley, and from there, you can go either way back to the street. Well, that's your escape route. You got that?"

Blankers nodded. It was simple enough. He was thankful that he wasn't afraid of heights, because a flight across rooftops and along narrow edges at this formidable altitude wouldn't be easy for somebody with a queasy stomach.

Suddenly something important occurred to him. "But if I lock my bedroom door and this little door as well, you and your wife won't be able to get out!"

The elderly gentleman smiled at him. "Don't worry about us. We've got our own escape route. Besides, we're too old to worry. What can the Germans do? Maybe shorten our lives by a year or two. Well, that's not much; it's a risk we'll have to take."

Blankers admired this elderly couple who were prepared to risk everything and expected nothing in return.

Gerritsen locked the trapdoor carefully. Together they walked through Blankers' little bedroom and back into the living room. In the meantime, Cor had disappeared. Blankers was about to ask what had happened to him, but checked himself. The less he knew about things that were none of his business the better. It was a rule he had taught others, and he knew enough to live by it himself.

Oom Koos didn't tell Blankers any more than was necessary either. One of those necessities included learning how to open the iron door to provide access to the warehouse. He took Blankers to one of the windows of the room. The pane was hidden by the leaves of plants and flowers, making it almost impossible for anybody to see in.

At first the carpenter saw nothing but houses and rooftops, but Oom Koos then showed him a small, round mirror that had been fastened to the outside of the window frame. It was positioned in such a way that the large metal courtyard door could easily be seen.

"That door is always locked," explained Oom Koos. "When friends come, they're supposed to give the prearranged signal: a couple of short blasts on the horn followed by a couple of long ones, or, if they come on foot, a couple of loud bangs followed by a few softer raps.

"We often change the signal. Right now, it's three short ones followed by two long ones. That's Morse Code for the number three, as you probably know. When we hear that signal, we take a look through the window. If the coast is clear, we pull the lever that's off to the right of the window. It has a long cord on it that goes all the way down to the door and operates the bolt. The only problem is that my hearing isn't what it used to be and neither is my wife's. Every once in a while we miss the signal.
That can be both inconvenient and dangerous. So you keep your ears open and alert us in case we don't hear it."

Blankers readily agreed; he was happy to be able to do something in return for the hospitality and generosity of these people.

Time rushed past and Blankers decided to go to sleep early. The strange day and his frayed nerves had made him tired. But he was intensely grateful for his deliverance, which had come at a time when he was sure he was going to die.

He recalled Psalm 62, which calls God a high tower for the oppressed. He had literally found such a high tower himself, way up in the attic of this enormous warehouse. But what protected him, he realized, was not the warehouse but God Himself. So before he slept, he knelt down to express his gratitude to God for his timely escape.

During the next few days Blankers met all kinds of people. Both

48

men and women showed up at very strange times to pay a visit to Oom Koos and Tante Miep. The reasons for these visits weren't clear to him yet, but he realized that there was a lot going on in this warehouse that had to be kept absolutely secret.

Sometimes a few men would spend the night here; there were enough places in the warehouse to accommodate them. A week or so after he had arrived, Blankers discovered a large cellar underneath the building. It contained, of all things, an illegal printing press and a kind of clearinghouse for forged documents and identity papers. These were used to facilitate underground activities and to protect people from the German bloodhounds.

Blankers would have loved to make himself more useful. At first he was given only small chores to perform, but after a couple of weeks, he was entrusted with part of the printing press operation. There was also an illegal radio down there, so they kept up to date with all the war news and with what was going on inside the country.

He knew, of course, that if he were captured, his life wouldn't be worth a cent. That was true for all the others too. With or without his present involvement in all kinds of illegal activities, the Germans would undoubtedly kill him if they ever got their hands on him.

As soon as he arrived at the warehouse, he began to grow a mustache. Once the mustache was fully grown, Oom Koos supplied him with plain glass spectacles. How different he looked! He was photographed and his snapshot was affixed to a neatly forged identity card. The document identified him as Gerard de Wit. Blankers didn't exist anymore. Gerard de Wit was not to roam the streets at will. But if necessary, he could go out to run errands or perhaps participate in certain underground activities essential to the war effort.

CHAPTER SIX

AN ENCOURAGING LETTER

Meanwhile, back in the village a lot had happened. Shortly after Blankers' escape, three German soldiers ransacked his home. Mrs. Blankers, home alone with Tonni, got the scare of her life when the soldiers barged into her house. But when she heard why, she was overcome with happiness.

So her husband had escaped! She hadn't been informed yet. All of a sudden she didn't care a bit that the Germans turned everything upside down.

Of course they didn't find anything. They questioned Mrs. Blankers, tried to browbeat her, and finally packed her off in their car. She was taken to the Ortskommandant for interrogation.

Tonni began screaming when he saw that these evil men were going to take Mommy away. Mrs. Blankers hadn't expected this either. Who was going to take care of her children when they came home from school?

Just before the car pulled away from the curb, she shouted to Tonni to go to the neighbours. There was no time to make any further arrangements because the tires squealed and the car roared away.

Despite this shock, the brave woman remained unbroken; the most important thing was that her husband was free.

The Ortskommandant raged at her. He banged his fist on his desk and threatened to send her to jail or to a concentration camp if she refused to tell him where her husband was. But Mrs. Blankers remained very calm and told him the absolute truth. She just didn't know.

That seemed to take the wind out of the Ortskommandant's sails. He seethed and bellowed on for a while, but in the end even he was convinced. To her great astonishment, she was set free within an hour.

She made it home just in time to prepare lunch for the children. Tonni was greatly relieved to see his mom back again.

Mrs Blankers didn't bother telling the younger children what had happened, but later that evening she told Treesa and Jan everything. They were thrilled that things had turned out all right. Nothing serious had happened to Mother, and Dad had escaped, even though they didn't know how, or where he had been taken.

The Germans continued to search some of the other houses in town. They also visited the Kooiman farm. Kooiman had counted on that and had taken all the necessary precautions. Accordingly, the search turned up nothing.

The Ortskommandant was sorely disappointed. He could forget about his much-hoped-for promotion. Yet the whole thing had been made easier for him because the terrorist had not escaped from his jail. The much-vaunted Gestapo, he sneered, stupid idiots, always so high and mighty, always belittling the work of the Wehrmacht. He indulged in a gleeful little smirk when he thought about how those "supermen" had been set up! But it confirmed his suspicions that this Blankers was indeed a dangerous character. Otherwise they wouldn't have involved the whole Resistance movement to spring him.

The Ortskommandant would have to bide his time. He might get another chance yet. He'd instruct Jonas Krom to keep his eyes peeled and snitch on everything and everybody. Besides, Jonas wasn't the only one; there were a number of other fairly energetic and ambitious stool pigeons who might stumble across Blankers' whereabouts.

*   *   *

For the first two or three weeks, Gerrit Greven didn't set foot near the farmhouse. Under no circumstance should he arouse German suspicions.

Finally, one dark, dreary afternoon in late autumn, he did go to the farm. The Kooimans had been hoping to see him, although they understood why he delayed.

They were terribly curious to find out where Blankers was, but Greven told them he'd been sworn to secrecy. Suffice it to say that their friend was safe and in good spirits; the rest they would have to find out from him after the war.

Without disclosing any names, Greven told them the story of how Blankers had been spirited away from the Gestapo. That made Kooiman's day! In his mind's eye Kooiman could well imagine their raging fury when they discovered they'd been tricked.

God had heard their prayer; Blankers was free. Well, he was relatively free; you couldn't really speak of freedom these days, especially since the Germans were escalating their terrorism daily.

Fall was one dull, rainy day after another. It was becoming a tiresome, monotonous business for Kris and Jan to cycle to the city each morning on their dilapidated old bikes. Jan's depression was deepening. He couldn't figure it out himself. He should be happy that his dad had escaped the enemy.

Of course he was grateful, but this harrowing, uncertain existence made him despondent. They used to be able to roam through the marsh, discovering its beauty and secrets. That had been exciting. And he used to see his dad every once in a while. But now? One day was the same as the next. And if anything newsworthy happened, it was usually bad.

Living conditions in the western provinces deteriorated rapidly. There was very little food, clothing, or fuel, especially in the large cities. Everyone despaired about the coming winter. In Amsterdam the parks had been closed to the public to prevent the people from cutting down trees. In Rotterdam the Germans were carrying out one raid after another. The Germans had collected fifty thousand men and boys and transferred them to German labour camps. They had also begun to focus their attention on Amsterdam and the Hague.

The merciless Allied bombings of German cities continued. But this was also true of cities and railroads in occupied territories. Amsterdam headquarters of the Sicherheits dienst[15] and Wehrmacht headquarters of

---

[15] Safety Service

52

General Christiansen in Hilversum had both been bombed. But despite the setbacks, the Germans were determined to fight on. Hitler had rejected the very idea of surrender and had threatened to kill anyone who even dared to think of surrendering. If Germany lost the war, Hitler would drag everybody down with him, not merely the German people but also as many people as possible in occupied lands.

Hitler had given special instructions for the Dutch western provinces. If the Allies ever managed to cross the rivers and penetrate into the western provinces, all large public buildings and all bridges were to be blown up. All dykes and sluices were to be opened or cut. The Allies would find only a watery wasteland. The German fuhrer had decreed that liberation for the western provinces would mean annihilation.

Of course the Dutch didn't know what the German tyrant had planned for them, but many people had vague suspicions about it. And yet people continued to yearn for liberation even though it might have terrible consequences. It was better to have one final Armageddon than to rot away slowly, devoured by fear, hunger, and misery.

But there were no big, decisive battles, no Allied thrusts across the rivers. Only the southern provinces were liberated. The rest of the country would have to wait until next year. In the meantime, the Germans had gone on the offensive again, this time with an array of deadly missiles, including the V-1 and V-2 rockets.

Mrs. Blankers was having a hard time. She couldn't possibly care for her children the way she wanted to. Though the shortage of food was not as severe here as it was in the western provinces, their diet wasn't very nourishing. If Kooiman hadn't helped out on occasion, she doubted whether she would have made it.

She was very concerned about Jan. The boy was visibly worsening. He was very thin and listless. His daily struggles to get to school were taking a heavy toll, but that wasn't the only problem. Jan could no longer handle the emotional tensions of this prolonged suffering.

His work at school deteriorated. In class his attention often wandered, and at night, he was too discouraged to do his homework well.

Mrs. Blankers could well understand what he was going through, but she also felt Jan had to fight back. He had a good mind; it would be too bad if he fell behind because of lack of determination.

One night she asked Treesa to go to bed earlier than usual because she wanted to have a confidential talk with her son. She tried to refocus his attention on God's faithfulness and mercy. At least, she pointed out, they were still alive and even had enough to eat. His father had been freed in a most miraculous way. True, there were a lot of sorrow and worry in their lives, as was the case with everybody else, but the Lord would come to their rescue at His appointed time. She urged Jan to keep that in mind at all times. And if things became too much to handle, he would have to take his troubles to his heavenly Father. The liberation might well come very soon. And it would be a great delight and relief to his father when he found out that his son had stood the test.

That's how she tried to rouse him out of his despair.
She would have done anything to make things easier for him.
She forgot all about her own cares. At times such as this she felt she had to be both father and mother to her children. She had to keep Jan on the right track at any cost.

At first Jan was gloomy and didn't react. But gradually he came to realize that he had bottled up his sorrows and, as a result, had ignored his schoolwork. He knew this couldn't go on; after all, he had promised that he, as the oldest of the children, would be supportive of his mother. And now look what he had done. Instead of helping his mom he had simply become another burden to her!

He resolved that things would be different from now on. He promised his mother that he would give it all he had and that he wouldn't bottle everything up anymore. Finally, they prayed together that God would help them and soon bring an end to their afflictions. Then they prepared to go to bed.

As Jan went to lock the front door, he spotted a letter on the floor that had apparently been slipped under the door. There was no name or address on it, not even a stamp. Surprised and a bit alarmed, he picked it up. Who could it be from?

54

Quickly he walked back to the living room and gave it to his mother. She ripped it open, took out a piece of paper, and gasped in surprise. She recognized the handwriting.

The letter had no date nor place of origin. Blankers didn't write too much about himself. He only wrote that he was well and that they shouldn't worry about him. The rest of the letter was for Mrs. Blankers and the two oldest children. What Blankers wrote was designed to put their minds at ease and to encourage them to go on. He expressed the hope that the two oldest children were doing everything within their power to help Mother and to do their best in school and also help the other children. And, of course, he hoped that the liberation would come quickly and that they would be able to see each other soon after.

While she read the letter aloud, Mrs. Blankers had a hard time controlling herself, and Jan had tears in his eyes. It seemed his dad knew exactly what had been troubling him. It was simply amazing that that kind of a letter would come just now! Jan realized that it was the Lord's doing.

Who had delivered the letter? Anyway, the deliverer had wanted to remain anonymous. It didn't really matter. The important thing was that all was well! It was too bad that there were no more details about where Dad was, but clearly he didn't want to take any chances just in case the letter fell into the wrong hands.

They read the letter three times, each time trying to glean some more information out of it. Mrs. Blankers said that she would show it to Treesa the next day, and then she planned to hide it so thoroughly that not even the Germans would be able to find it.

When they went to bed, Jan felt relaxed and relieved for the first time in weeks. In fact, now that he had unburdened his heart, he felt that he didn't need any sleep at all. He suddenly felt so refreshed that he could have worked all night. Still, within five minutes he was fast asleep.

The next morning Mrs. Blankers was immensely relieved to see Jan's change of mood. He was cheerful as he walked out of the house and he was still cheerful when he came back. After supper he withdrew to a corner of the room to do his homework, working feverishly to make up for lost time.

With the short days and the continued curfew, it was no longer possible for Jan to visit the Kooiman farm at night. Instead, he threw all his energies into catching up on his schoolwork. It took him quite a while because he had missed a lot, but he was making good headway. And whenever he felt he was going to slip back into the old rut, he recalled his discussion with his mother and his dad's letter. And before going to bed each night he asked the Lord to help him.

Things had taken a turn for the better. In school, his marks improved noticeably, and at home, the younger children finally realized that they had a big brother who looked after their interests. All around him things improved; and Jan was probably most pleased of all!

56

CHAPTER SEVEN

TRIAL BY FIRE

One afternoon in early December, Kris and Jan were biking their way home. School had been dismissed early because a couple of teachers had been absent. One had been sick, but the other, Mr. van der Laan, their homeroom teacher, had been arrested by the Germans. Nobody knew exactly why, and all the students were very upset and angry. Mr. van der Laan was one of their favourites, an excellent storyteller who knew a lot about history and other countries.

All of a sudden he had disappeared, picked up by the Gestapo. There were some rumours that it had something to do with an illegal newspaper, that he had written some articles and had helped distribute the paper. If that was true he would probably be shot.

It was now about two weeks before Christmas vacation. Jan was no longer worried about his Christmas report card, for he had pretty well caught up with the others. But there were rumours that the school would not be reopened after the holidays because of a shortage of fuel. Already it was so cold in the classrooms that most students had trouble concentrating on their work.

Jan and Kris didn't mind going home early. They were both looking forward to the holidays. Then they wouldn't have to struggle back and forth to school each day. But the idea of not going to school at all anymore didn't appeal to them either.

When they were about halfway home, they heard airplane engines overhead. "They're English fighters," said Kris, as the boys watched them come up out of the south. They were approaching rapidly. For once, it was clear and sunny and the fighters could be seen easily. Probably they were based at one of the Allied airfields in the south and were flying over on a reconnaissance mission.

It didn't take long for three German fighters, alerted to the Allied intrusion, to fly in from the north. Soon all the planes were involved in an intense dogfight.

The airplanes zoomed through the sky like angry wasps, shooting with machine guns and cannon fire.

Jan and Kris dismounted to view the spectacle, a fascinating, absorbing drama. One plane would climb to gain altitude and then pounce on an enemy airplane flying below. To escape such an attack, the plane flying below would zoom close to the ground and then pull up quickly or else tree-hop across the landscape, trying to dodge the enemy's attack. Whoever was least skilled at this kind of game ran a big risk of not surviving it.

On the ground beneath, the world looked peaceful. The road and the fields on either side were completely deserted. The two boys were the only witnesses to the airborne confrontation. There was only one house in the area.

Jan and Kris didn't think about the danger until a couple of heavy branches fell near them. A hail of machine gun bullets had struck an elm nearby. Suddenly the boys realized this wasn't the safest place to be.

"Let's get out of here!" shouted Kris. They dropped their bicycles and dashed toward the ditch at the side of the road. They got down as low as they could, very close to the water. This didn't give them a lot of cover, but at least it was better than standing out in the open. The only other shelter was the house, but that was too far away.

Once they felt safer, they crawled back up to the top of the ditch to see what was going on. One of the German airplanes was attacking an English fighter. Apparently it got hit. It shuddered and began to lose altitude.

Would it come down in flames? The boys waited with bated breath. About fifty metres above the ground, the pilot regained control. The engines, missing badly, began to rev up again, and the machine responded to its controls. It just missed the treetops as it levelled out, and it was so badly damaged that it had to quit the fight. The airplane banked and disappeared off to the south.

Another English plane was already diving down for vengeance. Unaware of his peril, the German suddenly found himself attacked from above. His craft took a terrific pounding from British cannon fire. First there was a trail of smoke, followed by flames shooting out of the engine and the wing. Soon the aircraft became a huge torch hurtling toward the ground.

For a minute Jan and Kris thought the burning fireball would come right down on top of them. They huddled close against the bank of the ditch. There was no longer time to run away.

Then the danger for the boys was past. But the doomed aircraft dove straight for the nearby house.

The two boys, mouths agape, were appalled. They could see exactly what was going to happen. The next second the airplane crashed down on the rooftop. The tail section and a wing broke off, but the main body bounced off the house and came hurtling to the ground about two hundred metres behind the house.

Above, the dogfight had ended. Apparently the Germans had enough of it. They banked and sped off in a northwesterly direction. The two remaining English aircraft continued their reconnaissance mission to the northeast.

Kris and Jan hadn't yet recovered from the shock. From where they were standing, they could see the smoking, burning wreck out behind the little house. There wasn't a single part of the plane that was not in flame. They hadn't seen the pilot bail out, so they figured he must be dead.

Dead. Incinerated in a sea of fire. True, he was a German, and therefore an enemy. Still, he was a human being. Jan suddenly got sick to his stomach when he realized that awful truth, and Kris turned pale too.

What should they do now? They couldn't very well go to the plane because the heat would roast them. There was really nothing they could do.

Then Kris glanced back at the house and saw that the roof had caught fire!

He jabbed Jan in the ribs and said, "Look at the house!"

Suddenly their paralysis left them. They jumped up, grabbed their bicycles, and raced toward the house. Both were thinking the same thing.

There might be somebody in the house who needed help!

The fire on the roof was spreading rapidly. By the time the boys got to the house, nearly the whole roof was in flames. One of the dormer windows had shattered, and the draft filled the whole downstairs with hideous black smoke.

They threw their bicycles down and ran to the front door which, they discovered to their dismay, was locked. They ran around to the side of the house but found that the side door was locked too! The boys looked at each other hesitantly. "We can't get in," Jan said. "It looks to me like there's nobody home."

Just then, amid the crackling of the sparks and the roar of the fire, they heard a child wailing. The cry was coming from the living room.

"We've got to get in there!" Kris shouted excitedly. He picked up a board lying next to the house, smashed a window pane, and began to pull the glass splinters away.

Jan helped him and in the process cut his fingers pretty badly, but he never even noticed the blood. Finally Kris got such a huge sliver of glass stuck in his hand that he had to stop to remove it. Without waiting for Kris to finish, Jan crawled in through the window.

The living room was filled with smoke and it burned his eyes. For a few seconds he couldn't see a thing, but then he spotted a figure lying on the floor. It was a woman. One end of a ceiling beam had been jarred loose by the impact and had come down on top of her. Was she dead? There was no time to find out; there was at least one other soul that needed to be saved.

Finally he spotted the child, a little toddler, sitting slumped in a high chair by the table. It was a little girl with blond curly hair. Although the smoke was beginning to cut off his breath, Jan rushed at the child. Things were quickly worsening in the room; the broken window was drawing the flames down from the attic. Feverishly Jan tore at the straps holding the little child down in her high chair, yanked her out, and ran to the broken window.

Kris had just managed to remove the piece of glass from his hand and was about to climb through the window.

"Take her!" Jan panted. "There's a woman in here too!"

60

He thrust the child down through the broken window and lowered her into Kris' arms. But what was Kris going to do with her? He looked around and spotted a shed about ten metres away from the house. Fortunately, the wind was blowing the flames and the smoke in the other direction, so the shed was a safe place to leave the girl.

Once outside, the child began to revive and cry. She was frightened, but at least her cheeks were gaining normal colour again.

The shed door was unlocked. Inside, there were some gardening tools and some small farm equipment. There was also a large white rabbit looking curiously out of its cage at the intruders. In one corner of the shed was a pile of potatoes.

Off to the side there was some straw, a good place to leave the girl for the time being, Kris decided. He removed his coat and wrapped it around the little girl, tying the sleeves together so that she wouldn't kick herself free. Then he left, closing the door behind him, and dashed back to the burning house to help Jan rescue the woman.

Jan had gone back inside to see what he could do about the woman. He turned her over and was surprised to see how young she looked. Down her left cheek was a long, ugly cut. Her eyes remained closed.

Just as Jan was wondering whether she was still alive, her face quivered slightly. So she was still alive! If only he could get her out of here, she might still have a chance!

Jan tried to lift her, but even though she was very light, he could not lift her by himself. What had happened to Kris? Jan ran back to the broken window and yelled, "Kris, come out here! But Kris was nowhere to be seen. It would be impossible for Jan to get the woman through the window all by himself. Even with the two of them it might not be possible. He had to think of something else. He sucked fresh air into his lungs and went back into the room. The heat at eye level was becoming so intense that he had to stoop in order not to get burned or pass out.

With the heat increasing by the second, he dashed through the room to the door. The metal doorknob was so hot it burned his fingers, but when he opened it, he discovered a corridor. At the end of it was the front door. The key was still in the lock. He had to get her through here!

He went back to the woman, grabbed her under the arms, and dragged her into the hallway.

The oppressive heat and choking smoke were overcoming him. Jan gasped for air, but there wasn't any. Then he broke out in a fit of coughing that made matters even worse. He was afraid he might throw up.

Still he fought on, slowly dragging the woman behind him. If only he could get a breath of fresh air! He had to stop for a few seconds. He couldn't go on. He carefully lowered the injured woman to the floor and was just about to stumble back to the window, when the whole room started to whirl in front of his eyes. His hands flailed out, trying to find something to hold on to. Stumbling sideways and then back, he tripped over something and then fell. That's the last he remembered.

Just then Kris came back to the house. There was more smoke coming out of the window now than before. When he stuck his head through the opening, he was almost overcome by the heat. Was Jan still inside? Was he still bearing up in that choking atmosphere? That was impossible!

"Jan, where are you?"

There was no reply, only a crash and a sudden shower of sparks as a couple of blackened boards came falling down from the ceiling.

Kris' hesitation was only momentary. He knew that Jan was somewhere inside. Maybe he was dead already. How could anybody stay alive in there? Should Kris risk his life? Any second now the roof could come down!

But then the hesitation passed, and he knew that he couldn't leave his friend in there to die. "Help me Lord!" he blurted as he started to squirm through the opening.

Where was Jan? Kris couldn't see the woman Jan had mentioned. Hadn't he heard Jan properly, or had his friend already made his own way outside?

Suddenly a wooden cabinet began flaming brightly like a torch. The light penetrated through the billows of black smoke. Then Kris spotted Jan and the woman lying near the opening to the hallway. Both of them were unconscious. Or were they dead?

Kris saw what Jan had been planning. He'd been trying to make his way to the front door. Kris dashed passed the bodies down the hallway, turned the key, and threw the door wide open. A sudden gust of fresh, lifegiving air came into the hallway, momentarily driving back the smoke and heat.

First Kris carried Jan outside, leaving him a safe distance from the house. Then he returned for the woman. By then some of her blond hair had been singed. Grunting and groaning, he dragged her through the hallway to the front door. When he finally got outside, he could think only of breathing fresh air again, but then a sudden, deep concern for the woman came over him.

Jan had recovered and was sitting up, pale and coughing. When he saw Kris, everything came back to him. He had passed out and his friend must have saved him.

"Feeling better?" Kris asked.

"Not bad! And thanks a lot!" He still felt dizzy and nauseous, but he bucked up and helped Kris carry the woman to the shed.

The little girl was no longer crying. She was sucking her thumb and looking at the white rabbit in the cage. When the two strange boys came in it looked as if she might cry again, but then she spotted her mom. How strange to see her mom carried in like that!

"Mommy seep?"

Yes, Mommy was asleep. The question was, if she would ever wake up.

Jan spread out some of the straw on the ground, and the two boys put the woman down on it.

What now? The two boys looked at each other helplessly. Somehow they had to help the woman regain consciousness. But how?

Kris swung into action. "Stay here," he said. "I'll see if I can find some water."

He did; behind the house there was a cistern and beside it a pail with a rope. He quickly drew a pail of water and ran back to the shed.

The woman still hadn't moved. With a damp handkerchief the boys dabbed at the woman's face. She moaned softly and her eyelids quivered. She was still alive and appeared to be fighting her way back to consciousness.

As they were tending to the woman, the boys heard the sound of car engines drawing near. Jan looked through the window and saw two German army vehicles come roaring up the road toward the house.

They pulled up in front of the house, and about a dozen German Wehrmacht soldiers jumped out. They paid no attention to the house but made straight for the wreck. By now, it had been largely gutted by fire. All that was left of it was a heap of twisted, scorched metal.

The boys felt ill at ease having so many German soldiers around. There was no telling what they might do.

Someone else was coming down the road riding a bicycle. As he drew near, Jan saw that his face looked ashen and despairing. He dropped his bicycle and stumbled toward the house. By now, there was nothing left of the structure except a blazing inferno.

The man ran his hand through his hair and then passed it in front of his face. Jan realized right away who he was. He promptly forgot all about his fear of the Germans and quickly ran out.

"Are you. . . do you live here?" Jan probed. The man didn't seem to grasp the meaning of his question. He stared at the boy vacantly, his eyes full of horror and pain.

Pointing to the shed, Jan announced, "They're over there." The man's face was suddenly transformed. He bolted off toward the shed, yanked open the door, and cried out with joy when he saw his wife and little daughter.

The woman had just come to. She gave a painful groan, but when she saw her child and her husband, she looked almost serene.

Outside things were getting hectic; a fire engine had arrived on the scene and hoses were rolled out to the cistern.
At this point Jan and Kris decided to leave the three alone and slipped out to watch the firemen at work.

It didn't take long to see that the house was completely destroyed, burned right down to the foundation. Fortunately there was no danger that the fire would spread since there were no other houses around.

The boys had soon had enough of the fire and went back into the shed. In the meantime, the man had done all he could for his wife. She had recovered her senses completely and seemed to be doing reasonably well, but it looked as if she had broken a couple of ribs. Perhaps also her head injury needed attention.

The little girl was sitting on her dad's lap. The man was so happy that his wife and little girl had been spared that he didn't seem the least concerned about his house.

He explained that he was a farmhand and had been working out in the field when the German airplane came down. He had known right away that the plane had come down somewhere near his house. When he had seen columns of smoke rising, his anxiety had overcome him. He had jumped on his bike and made a beeline for home. There he had seen his worst fears confirmed and for a moment had believed that his wife and child had perished in the blaze.

Kris and Jan took turns telling their side of the story. When they got to the locked doors, the man nodded. "My wife is always afraid to be alone these days. We're so isolated out here. Once in a while German military vehicles come by, and they often stop for one reason or other. She doesn't like that at all, and that's why she nearly always locks the doors. But I can't tell you how thankful I am that you risked your own lives to save my wife and child. I'll never forget this, boys."

Overcome by emotion, the man extended his hand. His wife, though still weak, also thanked the boys. By now, they were feeling a little bit embarrassed, and they blushed when the father held up his little daughter to give them a kiss.

The boys quickly turned attention away from their embarrassment by attending to what was going on outside. More and more people, including a couple of policemen, had drifted in to see what was going on. It wouldn't be long before some curious soul would decide to take a look in the shed.

Suddenly Kris gave Jan a poke in the ribs. "Look there. Germans!"

Three German soldiers had returned from the wreck and were passing through the crowd that had come to gawk at the fire. The spectators couldn't help seeing the remnants of the burned-out airplane, but they had been careful not to go anywhere near it.

The soldiers started interrogating the spectators. But all of them only shrugged their shoulders. It was clear from their reactions that they knew nothing about the incident. The soldiers became abusive, but their foul manners got them nowhere.

"I think they're looking for people who witnessed the dogfight and saw the airplane smash into the house," Jan explained.

Kris nodded. "We're the only ones who saw it, but I'm in no mood to tell the Germans about it. Let's leave quietly."

Their beneficiary had heard what they said. "Boys," he said, "there's one more thing you could do for me. I think my wife has to have a doctor. My daughter and I can stay with the farmer I work for, but I think my wife will have to go to the hospital for a while. Can you get us a doctor?"

"Of course!" replied Jan. "There's an excellent one in town, Doctor Jager, and we'll go there right away. He'll be out here in no time."

The man wanted to thank them once again, but the boys laughed and said they'd already had too much praise. They stole a quick glance at the Germans outside, but they didn't seem to be interested in the shed. Jan and Kris quickly and quietly made their escape. Their bicycles were still where they had left them.

They pumped off toward town as fast as they could. It wasn't easy, especially not for Jan, who had trouble getting any speed out of that old contraption of his. Besides, he was still a little bit dizzy and queasy. He felt as if he'd been working for weeks without sleep. He looked frightening too; his clothes were burned and scorched, his hands were bloody and burned, and his face was covered with soot and grime. By comparison, Kris looked pretty good. But his hands and face were soot covered too, and his right hand was bloody from the broken glass.

At last they reached the village and went straight to the doctor's house.

The maid answered the door, looking shocked at what she saw. "Hey, what have you guys been up to?" she inquired.

Jan and Kris had other things to worry about. "We have to see the doctor right away!" replied Kris.

Fortunately, Doctor Jager was home. Much to the maid's disappointment, the doctor took the two boys into his office. The boys told him all about the airplane, the fire, the woman, and the child.

The old Doctor listened intently, and his perceptive, piercing eyes sized the boys up carefully.

When Kris had explained everything, the doctor nodded approvingly. "You're brave guys. But let me see your hands young man."

Jan held up his hands. The doctor walked over to the medicine cabinet, took out a jar of ointment, and put it into Jan's pocket. "You take this, no charge. Your mother will have to apply that to your hands and then wrap bandages around them. Tomorrow you're confined to bed, and for the next two days, you can't leave the house. I'll come by to check on you. And now, away you go! I'm going to help right away."

Immensely relieved, the boys headed for home. Whatever anyone thought of gruff old Doctor Jager, there was no doubt that he was a fantastic person. He would do everything he could for the injured woman.

CHAPTER EIGHT

IN GOD'S CARE

"I'll go home with you for a minute," Kris said. That was okay with Jan. He had dreaded the prospect of facing his mother. She had so many other things to worry about, and she would probably be scared by his looks.

And yes, the moment she saw her soot-covered boy with his clothes all tattered and singed, she bombarded him with anxious questions, but Jan was just too tired to reply. Instead, he sank into a chair.

Kris did the explaining. He told her exactly what had happened, emphasizing the heroic role Jan had played. He also relayed Doctor Jager's message. Then he said goodbye, promising that he would visit regularly during the next three days.

Mrs. Blankers cleaned Jan's burns, dressed them, fed him some supper, and then promptly packed him off to bed. Then she looked after the rest of her children, who had also come home.

It wasn't until hours later that Mrs. Blankers could sit back and relax. The dishes were done and the children tucked in bed. In fact, she had even put Treesa to bed. She decided to step outside for a breath of fresh air and some meditation. Although curfew had already begun, the garden was relatively sheltered; no German could see her there.

There was a full moon, and the wind had picked up during the evening. Probably there was a storm coming; judging from the tattered clouds racing by overhead, it could be a violent one.

The lonely woman was thinking about her husband. Where could he be now? There was danger all around him. Would she ever see him again? Would there ever come an end to this dreadfully cruel war--an end to the storm that had raged relentlessly for more than four years over occupied Holland?

She was also thinking about her oldest son. What a hard time he'd had. Her husband's letter had done him a lot of good. But today she had again realized that during times like these, life was easily snuffed out. She had almost lost Jan. Suppose he had perished in the blaze? For a moment, her heart seemed to shrivel up inside her.

Actually, she had to admit that Jan had done well today. That made her very happy. She was also happy because God had protected him. In fact, God had spared all of them miraculously. Her husband had been snatched from the jaws of death. Now Jan had nearly gone through the fire but had escaped. And she too, as well as the other children, was healthy. They had a lot to be thankful for.

And she was indeed thankful, though sometimes her cares and anxieties weighed heavily on her, and she became preoccupied with them. This war was taking so long. And sometimes she felt very alone.

Then she looked up; she looked at the moon flashing out between the rapidly moving clouds. She looked at the stars silently blinking in the blackness above.

She vaguely recalled the words from one of the Psalms: "Praise the Lord. . . Who has made the great lights. . . The moon and stars to rule by night; for His mercy endureth forever."

She realized full well that the Lord was looking at her, even then. He knew her worries and those of her children. Their anxieties could still drag on for a long time yet, but God's goodness and His compassion would last much longer—in fact, through eternity!

She had aimlessly walked toward a tree in the garden, a maple. It had no leaves. The chilly damp, the long nights, and the biting, sometimes stormy wind had made it bare. The silvery moonlight caught the smooth twigs waving back and forth in the wind.

It was nearing the heart of winter, and there was a storm coming. Soon the cold would become almost unbearable, especially with so little fuel.

Deep in thought, Mrs. Blankers took hold of a twig that had been brushing her hair. Then by the sparse light of the moon, she saw that the twig was already full of buds. They were small, almost insignificant, but there was life in them, a life that awaited the resurrection of spring! That thought filled her with serenity; those tiny little buds assured her that spring would come. And so would peace and freedom. Throughout all the occupied territories, the signs of the coming liberation were multiplying.

"Praise the Lord. . . for His mercy endureth forever."

Smiling serenely, Mrs. Blankers walked back toward her house.

CHAPTER NINE

AN ADVENTUROUS JOURNEY

For weeks now Blankers had been a refugee in the warehouse. He had come to know every nook and cranny of the building and almost every secret of its operation. This huge building right in the centre of the city was also the centre of all kinds of anti-German activities. Here the Partisans printed illegal newspapers, false identity papers, and ration cards. Hidden deep beneath the building were weapons that would someday be used in open conflict with the Germans. Here people of the Resistance forged various dangerous plans that would help the Allied war effort. And the warehouse was also a hideaway for an assortment of people who were hunted by the Germans.

Refugees usually didn't remain for long. This was kind of a halfway house, no more. Otherwise, the warehouse would soon draw the attention of the Germans.

Blankers was an exception. He made himself useful in the secret print shop, and he was so handy and pleasant that the Gerritsens loved having him around.

A deep trust grew between the elderly couple and the refugee. Blankers was always amazed at the uncomplaining dedication with which these two people accepted risks and faced danger. If the Germans ever discovered what was going on here, the two of them would come to a bad end. And yet, although they always remained careful, they never hesitated and hardly seemed to worry.

Blankers often wandered out beyond the warehouse compound. He usually waited until late afternoon, just before dusk. With his mustache, spectacles, different clothes, and perfectly convincing forged identity card he would not be recognized easily. The men of the Resistance always needed couriers. There were always packages to be delivered at specific addresses. Often they contained weapons, and the courier had to know the passwords. Sometimes illegal newspapers were delivered and then distributed by the people around town. Blankers usually dropped bundles off at specific addresses. It just wouldn't do for the warehouse to have all kinds of visitors. Sooner or later that would be fatal. By now Blankers was getting pretty skilled at the business of deliveries.

One drab, damp late afternoon Blankers left the warehouse for an address at the far end of town. This time he had to deliver some ration cards. They were for other refugees. Since he wanted to look as inconspicuous as possible, he didn't carry a package. He put the cards inside his pockets and inside the sweatband of his hat.

As usual, the streets were empty. People wanted to avoid the nasty bone-chilling wind. The only relief to the monotony was the dim light of a few windows. But if you stopped to look inside them you soon discovered that there were mainly empty boxes on display!

Blankers stopped in front of the window and suddenly remembered that it would soon be *Sinterklaasfeest*[16]. Would his wife and kids ever be surprised if he came home with presents! But, of course, he wasn't even going to see them, let alone bring them presents. Once he had risked sending a letter, but he knew he couldn't repeat that. If the Germans sniffed out his trail, not only his own life but the lives of many others would be in danger as well.

Presents. There was hardly any merchandise for sale! Unless, of course, you wanted to buy on the black market and were prepared to pay through the nose!

Nearly everyone bought something on the black market occasionally. Sometimes the need was just too great. But Blankers despised the men who ran the black market. They were enriching themselves at the expense of their fellow countrymen. They could deliver almost anything, and their

---

[16] Sinterklaasfeest is celebrated in the Netherlands on December 5, when Sinterklaas, a bishop from Spain, comes with presents. Many people in Holland keep the proper distinction between Sinterklaasfeest and Christmas.

best customers were usually Germans who could afford to resort to the black market to get what they wanted.

"Come on," he scolded himself, "move it!" He'd been standing at the window daydreaming for almost ten minutes. This was no time to think about home. He first had to get rid of the ration cards. He deliberated for a moment. If he cut through the alleys, he'd be able to make up for lost time.

As he rounded the corner, he almost ran into a German soldier coming from the other side. He just managed to get out of the way. The German grumbled something about the "dumme Hollander." Blankers managed to compose himself. Imagine if he had collided with the man! His coat pockets were full of ration cards!

He remained calm and walked on. He couldn't prevent his heart from racing. These slums were certainly depressing! However, within five minutes he had left that part of town behind.

He came to a much wider street with a tavern on the corner. The barmaid was just filling some glasses, and at one of the tables sat three men, each with a drink in front of him. They were busy discussing something or other. Blankers assumed they were black marketeers discussing the fortunes of their territory. As he looked through the window, he didn't watch where he was going.

Suddenly he tripped over something, fell forward, and came down hard on the bricks. For a few seconds he lay there slightly groggy, and then he sat up straight. Something warm was dripping down the side of his face—a trickle of blood.

Concerned, two of the men in the tavern came outside. "Had one too many, eh?" one of the men joshed. They helped him up, and when they saw the blood running down his face, they took him into the lounge. There they escorted him to the table where they had been sitting and pulled up a chair for him.

Recovering quickly, Blankers reached for his handkerchief to stop the bleeding. The helpful barmaid came over with some water and a towel.

In the meantime, the three men had discovered that their "friend" was definitely not drunk. In their own way they genuinely wanted to help

Blankers, but he didn't care much for the atmosphere here. Now that he was beginning to feel better, he would have been happy to leave, but he didn't want to offend these people. As he looked them over carefully, he became more convinced that they were indeed black marketeers. The men wore expensive clothes and rings, and from their talk, Blankers concluded that this was their territory.

"You need something to cheer you up," one of them said, grinning. "Come on boys, let's have another round. I'm in the celebrating mood. Marie, bring us four more of those!"

The barmaid brought them four glasses of clear liquid. Blankers wanted to refuse, but the helpful chap took one of the glasses and put it to Blankers' lips. He had no choice but to drink; almost immediately he regretted it, for the stuff burned harshly in his throat.

"Well, thanks very much!' he said and got ready to go, but the others wouldn't hear of it. First they wanted to make sure he had recovered completely. They judged that he probably needed another drink.

Blankers wasn't about to go through that again, but he didn't have the courage to just get up and walk out.

It was fairly warm in the tavern. One of the men offered to take Blankers' coat off, but he politely declined. Just suppose they spotted the ration cards in his pockets! Then he realized that he had lost his hat. It had probably fallen off and rolled away when he fell to the pavement.

One of the men got up to have a look. He was gone for quite a while. Blankers had decided that the hat was gone, when the man finally came back. In his left hand he was carrying the hat, and in the right he was clutching a bunch of ration cards!

Blankers thought he might go through the floor. They must have come out of the sweatband of the hat. This was catastrophic!

The man grinned smugly. "I hadn't expected this, my friend. So you're one of us!"

One of them? The other two partners began to chuckle.

"Let's see. . . a tobacco card, a textile card, three food cards. . . well, well, you're not a wholesaler are you? Wow, this is a pretty good haul! But don't worry, we're in the same business and we won't rat on

74

you." Still chuckling, the man tossed the cards on the table in front of Blankers.

At last Blankers realized that they took him for a fellow black marketeer. Well, he'd have to play the role. They would not, of course, turn one of their co-workers over to the police. That was his only chance.

He quickly picked up the cards and stuck them in his pocket, mumbling, "Thanks boys, but keep it under your hat. And don't lose your hat the way I did! It's a pretty tough business, as you well know."

That broke the ice. The four men put their heads together and talked conspiratorially about all kinds of "addresses," presumably the addresses of customers and suppliers. They were being very careful about what they said because they knew they were competitors in the same business. But

Blankers got the distinct impression that the German Wehrmacht was one of their best customers. That made him even more cautious.

His "buddies" expected him to confide in them too. So Blankers tried to make do with all kinds of obscure references. When the men asked him where he lived, he replied that he came from another town and was staying with acquaintances for the time being. The other three members of the group were quick to discover that Blankers was a novice in the field. Still, they were ready to do business with him. At that point, Blankers got up quickly, thanked his benefactors once more, and disappeared from the lounge.

He breathed a sigh of relief when he shut the tavern door behind him. Good grief, he thought to himself, that could well have been the end of me!

He had to hurry; he felt like running, but that would probably look suspicious. Finally he reached a street corner from which he could no longer see the tavern. He kept going until he came to a wide shopping street which was busier than the part of town he had just left behind. At last he could relax.

His nose was no longer bleeding; the skin on his cheek was broken and there was some blood on his coat; but for the rest he hadn't done too badly. Anyway, that fall hadn't been the worst of it. How right those guys had been! He was inexperienced, even though his job was a bit different than they had imagined. But he would never risk going out like this again, not with a whole bunch of loose ration cards in his pockets!

His new friends hadn't suspected a thing. Or had they? Suddenly he felt that he was being followed. It was almost dark, but not far away there was a man who looked suspiciously like the one who had retrieved his hat and ration cards. Blankers couldn't be entirely sure because daylight was fading fast. He turned another corner and after about five minutes checked to see if the man was still there.

Sure enough, he was still about the same distance behind! Blankers no longer had any doubts. One of the three men had tailed him to see what he was up to and where he was going.

He had to shake the man somehow. Maybe he was suspicious that his alleged "colleague" was really a member of the Resistance. Then again, it might simply be curiosity. But in any case, Blankers refused to compromise his mission.

But what to do? One thing was sure: he had to change direction immediately and not proceed to his destination.

He took the first sidestreet left and then the next one right. Then he bent down, pretending to tie his shoelace. The black marketeer was still behind him.

Blankers forced himself to be calm; there had to be some way to get rid of that shadow. The trouble was, he didn't know this part of the city very well, and the spy probably knew it like the back of his hand.

He went on, looking for another opportunity. But he was determined to bypass his destination as long as that fellow was dogging his footsteps. And he wouldn't go back to the warehouse either!

He rounded another corner. A fire route corridor ran parallel to a row of houses, the fronts of which faced the street Blankers had just come from. He bolted down the length of the fire route as fast as he could. At the end of it was another fire route perpendicular to it, leading back to the street. He stuck his head out into the street and spied both ways to see if he could catch a glimpse of his pursuer, but the man was no longer there.

Across the street there was a door leading to another fire route. Quickly he crossed the street, tried the latch, and opened the door. Blankers was sure that by now he had lost his tail. But when he came out into another street he didn't know exactly where he was anymore.

He didn't want to inquire, and, anyway, there was hardly anybody on the street. He would just have to keep going until he got to familiar territory. All the while he kept a sharp lookout just to make sure that his "colleague" hadn't picked up his trail again.

After a while he came to a wide shopping street that he recognized. He slipped into the dark doorway and contemplated what to do now. Having made his decision and making sure of his bearings, he walked off again, moving quickly because he had lost a lot of time. The uneasy feeling hadn't vanished entirely, but there were no further incidents. Apparently he wasn't being followed anymore. Finally he reached his destination.

CHAPTER TEN

LUDWIG'S BIRTHDAY!

The destination was a simple house in a working class district. A woman of slight build and a very pale face opened the door. She eyed the visitor suspiciously.

"You have a dog for sale?" Blankers asked.

A look of recognition sparkled in the woman's eyes. "That's right!" she replied.

"What breed is it?"

"It's not a German Shepherd; it's a Scottish Terrier."

That was the recognition code, and Blankers was certain he was at the right house. "I've got the ration cards," he said softly.

"Come on in." The woman escorted him to the living room where her husband was, a young man with sharp eyes that studied the visitor carefully.

Blankers immediately pulled out the ration cards; there wasn't much time to talk. He had to get going if he wanted to make it back to the warehouse before curfew.

Minutes later he was back outside without the ration cards. They hadn't weighed much, but he felt about twenty kilograms lighter! Now he just had to be careful not to run into one of his dedicated "colleagues"! He resolved to steer clear of the route he had taken earlier. He made it back to the warehouse just before curfew.

Oom Koos and Tante Miep had two visitors. One of them was Cor, the man who had driven the getaway car. He visited the warehouse quite often since he was a member of the active Resistance group whose headquarters was in the warehouse cellar.

The other man was a stranger; he introduced himself as Jansma, but Blankers knew right away that that probably wasn't his true name.

Jansma was a tall young man. His decisive attitude and mannerism betrayed military background. Before long, Blankers knew quite a bit more about this newcomer. He had just come from England! Two nights before he had been parachuted in to take up contact with the Resistance.

Their guest had much news about conditions in England and in the rest of liberated Europe. He was sure that the war would end sometime in the spring. Allied armies were continually being reinforced and re-equipped, while German reserves were dwindling rapidly.

In turn, Cor briefed Jansma about conditions in the Netherlands. Jansma had brought in a transmitter for sending messages to England. Later that night he got it going and established contact with headquarters in London.

Two days later there was a meeting in the Gerritsen living room. Cor was present, as were Willem, who had assumed leadership, Dijkmans, Heins, and Meijer. Blankers, now known as Gerard de Wit, was also part of it. They listened to the plans Jansma was outlining for them.

Within the next few days, a British airplane would be making a weapons drop at a prearranged location. It would be their job to pick up the weapons and transport them to a secure place.

The date hadn't been determined yet. The signal, to be radioed out from London, would be the cryptic message, "Today is Ludwig's birthday." The weapons would be dropped that same night. The men would have to make sure that they were at the field in plenty of time. The field was about twenty kilometres outside the city. Willem, who knew the area very well, gave his men instructions. They would be leaving the next day and would wait in an isolated farmhouse close to the field. Part of the weapons would be hidden on the farm while the rest would be smuggled back to the city and stashed in the warehouse. The British government thought it important to arm local resistance movements just in case hostilities erupted in these parts.

Jansma himself would not be present at the weapons drop. He had other things to do.

Blankers found it impossible to sleep that night. He didn't like the city, even though he was very thankful for the refuge he had found here. He had been longing to be out in nature again, even if only for a couple of days. This kind of activity was very dangerous. If caught, you got the firing squad. But the prospect of danger didn't bother Blankers. He had gotten used to that. Besides, he was happy to have a distraction from his otherwise monotonous existence.

At about 10:30 the next morning Blankers heard the signal he had been waiting for: three long blasts on the horn of a car that had just pulled up in front of the main gate.

He said goodbye to the Gerritsen couple and hurried to the entrance. There Blankers saw a van with a methane-fired generator installed at the rear. Cor was sitting behind the steering wheel.

Apparently looking forward to the little caper, Cor laughed cheerfully and invited Blankers to sit up in front with him. They would pick up the others as they went out.

When Cor started the engine, Blankers was surprised to see that it was using ordinary gasoline. Seeing the astonished look on his companion's face, Cor burst out laughing again.

"That generator is just to fool the Germans! I've got all the proper papers for the car, but it's almost impossible to get gasoline anymore. So we supposedly use methane, but that's just between you and me. By the way, if we're stopped, let me do the talking. I've been through all this before."

Blankers merely nodded; he knew that Cor was competent. He remembered how Cor had talked himself out of the roadblock after the jail escape.

Presently they picked up Willem and Meijer and after that Heins and Dykmans. All four men sat in the back of the van.

They drove straight to the farmhouse, where they would stay until the signal came through. After passing through some woods, they came to open fields and pasture land. Even though it was drizzling and dark, Blankers still enjoyed this trip out in the open.

This time they were fortunate; there were no roadblocks. At long last they reached a village and passed through it to get to the farmhouse. It was a large house named Fairview set quite a way back from the road. The house was suitably named; from there you could look far out over the countryside. The surrounding land was flat and unbroken, except for occasional rows of trees along sideroads or ditches.

Farmer Veltman and his wife were past middle age and they had three sons and a daughter, all grown up. One of the sons was married and living in a house not far from the farm. The Veltman couple apparently knew what this was all about. They didn't ask any questions at all. The car was parked in one of the sheds behind the house, and the six men proceeded to the large farm kitchen where the farmer's wife and daughter were preparing a meal for them.

Late that afternoon, the six men went to the barn and the shed to help with the chores. Willem and Blankers had milked before, and since Fairview was a dairy farm, they could make themselves quite useful.

Blankers felt right at home on the farm. He hadn't enjoyed himself like this for ages. For the first time in months he actually felt like whistling and joking.

That evening they all listened with excitement to the English broadcast. While fascinated to hear about the course of the war and the continuing degeneration of the enemy, they were more anxious to hear whether the secret message "Today is Ludwig's birthday" would be signalled through.

But the message didn't come. Somewhat disappointed, the six men looked at each other in silence. Blankers suddenly realized that he was a bit relieved. At least they would be able to stay here another day!

The Veltman family retired early; the six Resistance men bedded down in the hay. Blankers couldn't fall asleep right away; he caught himself thinking back about what had happened that day. After supper, Veltman had read a chapter from the Bible. After that he had said a prayer asking God to protect them all, especially during the risky business of picking up the weapons. His eloquent prayer had impressed them all, but especially Blankers.

Next to Blankers lay Willem. He too, was still awake, though not because he was tense or anxious. He was an old hand at this sort of thing. He came from somewhere in the north, or so it seemed from his speech. He had been an active member of the Resistance for two years now. At first he had been a member of an active Resistance squad elsewhere, but all the other squad members had either been killed or taken prisoner. He didn't seem to be afraid of anything and had no dependents other than his mother. In that sense, risks were a lot easier for him than for Blankers, who was often preoccupied with his wife and children.

"Can't you sleep, man?" Willem asked, noticing that his neighbour was tossing and turning.

"Not just yet. You too?"

"I don't need much sleep. Five, six hours is enough for me. It's not bad here actually. I've had a lot worse on some of the other outings we've had."

"Tell me about it," replied Blankers, anxious to find out what actually happened during one of those capers.

Usually Willem wasn't very talkative, especially not about his role in the Resistance, but for some reason tonight was different. In a hushed tone he told Blankers about some of his experiences. About cold, unending nights spent in the woods or the open field. About hunger and exhaustion, about schedules gone awry and about the sudden appearance of German troops and the resulting skirmishes. Not that Willem had experienced them all; some of them were adventures his friends had told him about.

"No, compared to some of that, this is a pretty soft touch: good food, excellent care, and a fine place to sleep!" he concluded, smiling. And Blankers had to agree. Today had been one of his better days. But who could know what lay ahead?

Blankers didn't fall asleep until much later, but he made up for it by sleeping in. When he looked at his watch, he started. But he quickly discovered that his comrades-in-arms were either still asleep or talking softly with each other. And why not? They had all the time in the world. Only Willem was gone.

Half an hour later they were all sitting around the breakfast table enjoying a very special treat: homemade bread and fresh milk from the morning milking.

At 1:15 that afternoon Willem tuned in to Radio Belgium. It was a French-language broadcast and was difficult to follow for most of the men, but the news was followed immediately by coded messages, some of which were in Dutch.

The men listened tensely, but the broadcast passed without giving their message. The receiver crackled, and Radio Belgium seemed to go off the air. Was this the end? No, there was more to come; then, finally and quite clearly, "Today is Ludwig's birthday!"

The excited men laughed and slapped each other on the back. This was it! The only one to keep his cool was Willem.

"This is only an advanced message," he explained. "It means we have to be prepared. At 8:30 tonight we have to tune in to Radio Orange. If the message is repeated, it means the airplane will come tonight. Unless, of course, somebody higher up calls it off; you never know for sure what they're doing up there."

Willem was right, of course, but the men were all keyed up and planned to stay that way. Now they had to get everything ready. One of the farmer's sons was sent into town to alert a group of fifteen trustworthy men to be prepared to move that night. Some of them would be given revolvers and posted to watch the access roads to the fields. Should the Germans show up, these men would be responsible for holding them off.

The field had been used once before. The farmer fetched a map of the area and spread it out in front of the six men. Now they would plan their approach.

They studied the map carefully. Each man was assigned a certain position and given a certain job to do.

Willem and Cor were the only ones who had revolvers. Willem would be in charge of the job, and Cor would be his second in command. Each of the other four men were given a powerful flashlight, two red and two white, which were to be used as signals. They were told to position themselves at the four corners of the field. The minute the airplane passed over, they had to flash out the Morse Code for the letter Z: two long flashes, followed by two shorter ones. The minute the parachutes had landed, they would each comb their sector of the field and, together with the men from the village, collect and secure the materials.

All the instructions were repeated once more; a lot depended on the success of this operation.

The farmer's son returned from the village and explained that everyone had been alerted and informed as to what was expected of them. Most of them had participated in the previous weapons drop.

It was late afternoon and dark was falling. To fight off the jitters, most of the men were sitting around chainsmoking. Their ration of cigarettes was quickly used up. To fill the remaining empty hours, the men pulled out their pipes. Farmer Veltman passed around some of his homegrown, home-cured tobacco. Soon the huge farm kitchen was filled with blue smoke. Jenny, Veltman's daughter, fled from the air pollution with disgust but soon returned to prepare supper for the men.

*   *   *

Anxious to find out whether the drop was on, the men congregated around the receiver well before 8:30. The unit had been stashed in a wall cabinet to make it as inconspicuous as possible, just in case the Germans or any of their henchmen showed up.

The farmer tuned in to the right frequency, and the audience fell silent.

First there was news, then a brief commentary on the news, and finally an analysis lasting fifteen minutes. Following that came the coded messages and suddenly: "Today is Ludwig's birthday!"

An audible sigh of relief went up from the group of men huddled around the receiver. This was it. Tonight was the night!

CHAPTER ELEVEN

THE ARMS DROP

Willem knew that the airplane would arrive sometime between ten o'clock and midnight. There was still lots of time. He checked everything over once more, including the weapons, the lanterns, and the compass. The men pulled out the map again. They also checked the wind direction, which would determine how they positioned themselves.

From far off came the sound of airplanes. The men started to get up, but Willem smiled. "It's much too early. They're destined for Germany. We've got lots of time."

At a quarter past nine they made their way out to the farm yard. There were eight of them: six Resistance men and Veltman's two sons. The third son had already gone to meet the people from the village and position them in their proper places.

The two sons rolled a wagon with rubber tires out of the barn. It would transport the heavy metal cylinders in which the weapons were shipped. The men would pull the wagon themselves because a horse would leave too many telltale tracks and possibly panic at the sound of an airplane passing low overhead. The men fetched some shovels and ropes and threw them onto the wagon; they might just need them.

At half past nine they started out, four men were in front pulling the wagon, three were pushing it, while one of the farmer's sons led the way.

It was pitch black, with not a star to be seen. Lanterns would have betrayed their whereabouts. And unnecessary noise was just as dangerous. You could never be sure if there was a German or a civilian policeman around.

They had a hard time finding their way in the inky blackness. After a while, they came to a gate leading to one of the pastures. The going was easier here because they didn't have to watch their step so carefully.

The grass was damp, Blankers noticed, his feet were getting wetter and wetter. His shoes had seen better days.

Back on the road, Blankers had been one of the four men pulling the wagon, but when they had moved into the pasture, they had changed positions. Now he was pushing, which was somewhat easier.

Next to him was Dijkmans; the two men talked softly.

Suddenly, Dijkmans' legs disappeared into a hole full of water. He fell forward, just managed to repress a scream, and thrust out his arms to break his fall. "Gerard, give me a hand!"

Blankers was already helping out. As he helped his partner up, he noticed that the man was soaked to the knees.

"Hadn't you better go back?" Blankers asked with concern.

"Are you nuts? Because of a bit of water? I've been through a lot worse. No, I want to be part of this." He wrung out the bottom of his trousers the best he could and then removed his shoes and socks to try to dry them a little bit too.

The delay cost them only a few minutes. Now they suddenly realized that their mates, not having seen what happened, had simply gone on. They were all alone in this world of darkness. They didn't dare call out; Willem had given them strict orders not to make any unnecessary sound.

"I remember the wind came from the left," observed Blankers. "Come on, we'll catch up with them."

They walked off briskly. Suddenly they were startled by something that jumped up in front of them and dashed off.

"A rabbit," Dijkmans growled. "Scared the wits right out of me."

Presently they were at the edge of a deep ditch. It was clear by now that they were on the wrong track. The wagon couldn't possibly come this way. Blankers was still convinced that he had been on the right track, but the wagon could have changed course. What now?

Suddenly they heard an owl hoot in the distance. It sounded so natural that Blankers was fooled for a moment. Then he recalled that Willem was good at imitating owls and that this was the prearranged signal for lighting the lantern.

Relieved, both men turned toward the sound. They spotted a dim light flashing on and off in the distance. One of Willem's men had lit the lamp to show their whereabouts.

Blankers signalled back with his own flashlight by holding the light inside his coat and turning it on only briefly. The two men quickly jogged off in the direction of the light. After a couple of minutes they had rejoined the group, much to their own relief.

At first, Willem was pretty upset. In a low voice he gave them a severe scolding. It was careless of them to fall behind, he lectured. They had jeopardized the success of the whole operation. Willem hadn't wanted to use the light just in case there were unfriendly eyes around.

Blankers explained what happened and assured Willem the delay had been unavoidable. The explanation seemed to satisfy the group leader, and he checked his anger. "Let's make sure we stay together! Otherwise, in this darkness we'll all get lost," he cautioned once more. "Now let's go."

Soon they came to a second gate, which was being guarded by the farmer's youngest son and the assistants from town.

The men exchanged a few words and made sure that everything was all right. Guards had already been posted on the access roads. If anything went wrong, the men picking up the drop would have plenty of warning.

88

On they went for another five minutes, this time on a path through the field. They crossed a dam across a deep ditch. Presently their guard halted and whispered, "This is it."

Willem gave his final instructions. The men were to spread out across the field to their prearranged positions, keep quiet, and keep their eyes open.

The three men with flashlights were positioned in a straight line, parallel with the wind, about a hundred metres apart. The first man had a red lamp, the second a white, and the third another red one.

Blankers was the fourth man. He was assigned a position about fifteen metres to the side of the third man. His lamp was white, and he was supposed to signal the letter Z in Morse Code.

By now all had taken their positions. It was ten o'clock.
All they could do was wait for the English airplane to come, if it came at all. . .

Willem walked back and forth across the dark pasture. Either he had excellent night vision or he had an infallible sense of direction, because he had no trouble locating each man on the field. Not until he had made sure that everyone was in position did he begin to relax.

Time passed slowly. Blankers' feet were ice cold; he paced back and forth a little to keep the circulation going, but he didn't dare wander far from his assigned position.

Overhead, the cloud cover began to break up. By the subdued light of the few visible stars, the field took shape. Picking up, the wind blew cold on Blankers' cheek. He shivered and put the collar of his jacket up.

From far off came the roar of airplane engines. The men tensed up.

Nearby, anti-aircraft batteries opened fire, tracer bullets drawing fiery lines into the dark skies above. The white beams of searchlights flashed through the openings in the cloud cover, seeking prey. Less than twenty kilometres away, a bitter conflict developed between the flak installations and the British bombers overhead.

Near the field there were no anti-aircraft batteries. That was one of the reasons this spot had been selected. The airplane making the drop had to come down to a low altitude, where it would be a sitting duck for the German flak.

Suddenly Willem popped up beside Blankers. Calmly he reminded Blankers, "Remember, Gerard; don't give the signal until you hear me hoot."

"I got it!" Blankers tried to sound as calm as Willem, but he couldn't deny the anxiety within.

The drone of airplane engines grew louder. Willem listened intently.

"There are also a couple of nightfighters around," he murmured. "That's not going to make it any easier."

Blankers knew what he meant. Nightfighters were very fast German airplanes that specialized in attacking bomber formations. The formation didn't fly right overhead but veered to the north. The flak batteries ceased firing, and the searchlights were turned off.

Willem walked away, leaving Blankers alone feeling disappointed. Why hadn't their airplane come?

Shortly after, he heard the sound of an airplane coming from the northeast. Was it a German fighter returning from pursuit? Or was it their airplane?

The roar increased as the airplane seemed to fly right at them. Should they turn on the lights now or not? Was that pilot a friend or a foe? Well, Willem would have to decide. But how would he know?

Judging from the sound, the airplane had banked. It flew by toward the west. Had they botched it? Then they heard the airplane bank again, and presently it came straight at them. This was almost unbearable! When was Willem going to signal?

Then Blankers heard the hoot of an owl! The lights went on. Blankers aimed his flashlight at the airplane and flashed the prearranged signal: two long dashes followed by two short ones.

Had the pilot seen it? Yes indeed! By way of confirmation, the airplane began to descend. The noise was deafening! The planes bomb bay was open, and the men on the ground could see light shining out through it. Then they saw something drop as the airplane passed directly overhead.

Within seconds, Blankers spotted a number of long, cylindrical objects dangling at the end of open parachutes. That must be what they had been waiting for.

90

The airplane engine revved up again, and the aircraft banked to make another pass. Apparently he had dropped only part of his cargo.

Once again Willem hooted like an owl, and again the lights were turned on. Blankers flashed the Morse Code, and a second load was promptly dropped.

Just as the British airplane revved up and started to gain altitude, they heard another airplane approaching—probably a German fighter.

The English bomber, having dropped its cargo, disappeared at top speed; but the other craft circled overhead.

"Get down!" Willem shouted. Immediately all the men dropped flat and motionless in the grass. It was a good thing too, because the next moment the German pilot had dropped a flare that illuminated the whole area. Fortunately the flare wasn't directly above them but several hundred metres off to the right. Still, the men felt exposed; they thought for sure they would be discovered.

The German plane circled overhead and then dropped a second flare somewhat further away. None of the men dared move, but gradually it looked as if they would escape detection. The burning flare floated in the air for several minutes, but to the men, it felt like several hours. They had to collect and secure the weapons, and there wasn't much time. When the last of the flares died out and darkness returned,, the German airplane banked and disappeared. Getting up, Blankers noticed that his teeth were chattering. Was that due to the cold or the tension?

Immediately Willem swung into action. "All right, get up! The danger is past. But we have to get a move on. The Germans are up to something. They may send soldiers to investigate. We have to secure the weapons as quickly as possible."

The men started working as quickly as their stiff joints would allow. It felt good to be back in motion and getting warmed up. They combed the field; most of the containers were quite easy to spot because of the attached parachutes. The containers were very large indeed; about two-and-a-half metres long, with a diameter of sixty centimetres. On the bottom of each container was a kind of cushion that acted as a shock absorber.

Secured to each of the cylinders was a shovel. That was to bury both the cylinders and the parachutes if necessary. But not this time. Everything had to be loaded onto the wagon and taken back to the barn.

The containers were so heavy it took five men to carry one of them. For the next half hour the men worked so hard that no one was troubled by the cold.

When the whole field had been thoroughly searched, they had found eight containers. But Willem wasn't satisfied.

"There should be ten of them," he said decidedly. "Two of them probably drifted off."

There was nothing to do but to search the adjacent fields. And Willem turned out to be right; one container was found in a ditch and the other right in the middle of an elderberry bush. The parachute was all tangled up in the branches, and it took them quite a while to free it because they had to be careful not to leave any telltale signs behind.

It was well after midnight before they had assembled everything. Time was getting short, and a lot had to be done yet. The men quickly teamed up to move the wagon out. With such a heavy load, the rubber tires were essential. Some of the men pulled while others pushed, and this time the people from the village helped too.

The going was pretty rough, but at least it wasn't as dark as it had been earlier. They finally arrived at the farm, and all of the men, though very tired, were happy that everything had gone without a hitch.

The Veltmans weren't asleep yet; the farmer came out to meet them and ask them how things had gone. The wagon was driven into the rear of the house, the area that used to be a threshing floor, and Mrs. Veltman and her daughter came in with hot milk for the half-frozen conspirators.

Then they opened the containers. Some of them held smaller containers of munition, hand grenades, and various other kinds of explosives. Other containers had larger weapons, such as machine pistols, rifles, and stenguns.

When everything was unpacked, the empty containers were taken outside and buried.

Inside, the men worked by the light of a couple of lanterns. The windows had been carefully covered with black paper. All the access roads to the farmhouse were being watched by guards who would alert people in the farmhouse if anything went wrong.

First the men organized the pistols, explosives, fuses, hand grenades, incendiary bombs, and some items they had never seen before. But there were detailed instructions concerning each type of weapon.

One container was completely filled with treats--sugar, chocolate, cigarettes, biscuits, and much more.

It was the food that made Blankers feel that he was living in a fantasy. He had to pinch himself to make sure he wasn't dreaming. Suddenly this grey December night held a promise of things to come--the new spring and the ultimate liberation. Many of the weapons were buried in an underground cellar that was as secure as anything could be. From time to time the Resistance would pick up parts of the supplies to be distributed among the various local squads.

Willem supervised the classification of materials. Often he selected certain weapons and boxes of ammunition, explosives, and other tools of the sabotage trade to lay them aside to take to the city later. That trip back to the city would have its perils, but that couldn't be helped.

The whole business of unpacking and repacking took hours. Most of the larger weapons had been shipped disassembled and first had to be reassembled. And some of the items were so touchy that they required maximum care.

Willem sent a couple of village men to check with the guards to see whether there were any problems. Fortunately, everything was still quiet.

When they were at last finished with the weapons, they started dividing up the food. The men from the village were given their share, and the rest was earmarked for the Resistance squad in the city. Farmer Veltman himself declined any of it. Life on the farm wasn't that bad yet.

It was half past three in the morning when they had finished. There remained only the stuff that had to be taken back to the city. The six men from the Resistance would load that up. The town people rested in the hay for a while. Curfew didn't end until five A.M., and that's when Veltman would call them. They would then find separate ways to town.

Loading up the van wasn't simple. They couldn't simply chuck the stuff in the back. That would be looking for trouble.

Veltman had a solution for that. On his dairy farm, he also grew his share of potatoes and vegetables. His sons fetched wooden crates and boxes from the barn. The men wrapped the weapons in paper and hid them in the boxes under layers of Brussels sprouts, cauliflower, and potatoes. Finally they loaded everything into the van. They put the larger weapons into burlap bags which they topped with potatoes.

Would the camouflage do the trick? Well, it wouldn't stand up to a really vigorous search, but they had to risk it. Cor would drive, and he could talk his way out of almost anything. Besides, he was armed with all kinds of impressive papers signed by the Wehrmacht. Who knows, they might get away with it. And if they were caught, well, those who knew something about guns would try to shoot their way through. They weren't going to be caught like sitting ducks.

CHAPTER TWELVE

"CAN'T STOP!"

At five A.M. the men from the village were awakened. Within minutes they left, each in a different direction.

Willem hesitated, wondering whether he and his own people should leave now. It was pitch black and foggy outside. His men were dead-tired, having worked through most of the night.

He talked it over with Veltman, who advised him to wait. If German soldiers were sent out to look for weapons, they wouldn't do so until the break of dawn anyway. Moreover, the farm would be alerted by telephone in case something went wrong. In the nearby German garrison, there were a couple of German soldiers who could be relied upon to tip them off. The farm was usually informed well before any military action was taken. That had happened before; Veltman would be tipped off, and he, in turn, would call up the places where the raids were scheduled to be carried out.

All the men of the Resistance squad, except Willem, fell down in the hay and were fast asleep immediately.

Two hours passed, but then, at seven A.M. Veltman's telephone rang. Veltman hadn't gone to bed, half expecting a telephone call. After a brief discussion, he went to the shed and found that Willem was already up and ready to go.

"It's time to go," said Veltman softly. "The Germans are coming. A whole platoon is going to search the fields, and they've also been ordered to stop and examine every vehicle on the road. You'd better leave right away."

Willem nodded; he now regretted not having left at five o'clock. They might have avoided this! He quickly went around to awaken the men. Five minutes later they were ready to go, though still a bit wobbly on their feet. Each was given a sandwich to take along. Then they said goodbye to the Veltman family. Willem and Cor sat up front in the van while the other four crawled into the back among the crates of vegetables.

The doors were slammed shut. Cor revved up the engine, and the van took off.

It was still fairly dark and foggy. The back doors of the van had a couple of windows so that the men in the back could see outdoors.

After a while, Blankers noticed a number of small holes that had been drilled in the back doors and the sides of the van. They were covered with round metal disks that could be slid aside. When he' moved one of the disks aside with his finger, he was surprised at how thick the van walls were.

"Peepholes?" he asked Dijkmans, who was sitting beside him.

Dijkmans chortled. "It all depends. If the Germans stop us, we tell them we work for Food Administration. Right now we're carrying a shipment of vegetables for the city, and those holes are to let fresh air circulate through the van. That way the vegetables stay fresh."

"You think they'll swallow that?" Blankers asked doubtfully.

"Oh, a lot of them are stupid enough to swallow anything. But you need only one who doesn't. Once they inspect the van, they'll find out soon enough that the walls have been reinforced, and once they know that, they'll find the weapons soon also. Then they'll also know that those holes aren't for looking through or for fresh air, but for shooting!"

Astonished, Blankers fell silent. At last the gravity of the situation struck home. They were in some sort of an armed car loaded with weapons, and they might well have to fight their way through a number of roadblocks.

"I don't even know how to shoot," he said helplessly.

"Well, it's time you learned, Gerard! One of these revolvers will be for you, if we get out of this alive, and then you'll learn quick enough. Right now it doesn't matter so much. A couple of sharpshooters is all we need right now. See that big crate at the back! In it are two machine guns ready to go. Of course I hope it won't be necessary. We're making pretty good time."

But just then, up front, the look on Willem's face changed from

96

contentment to downright worry. About a hundred metres down the road two men got up from the side of the road and signalled them to stop. They were carrying guns.

"Rats, civilian police! They're everywhere, and they're worse than the Germans," he growled.

Cor nodded agreement. Besides, these weren't military men or city people, and so they probably wouldn't go for the story about airholes and food administration. Well, they had to try it.

They stopped and the two men walked up to the cab. One of them was pointing his gun at Cor's head, and the other demanded to see their papers.

Cor rolled down the side window, suddenly sporting an N.S.B. pin on the lapel of his coat.

"Heil Hitler, comrades!" he chortled cheerfully. "You're up early. That's a good thing too, because there are a lot of strange things going on these days." He took out his wallet with all the formal documents and handed it over to the policeman.

Seeing the N.S.B. pin and the official papers, the man suddenly became more amiable, but he studied the permits and documents carefully nevertheless.

"Is something the matter, friend?" Cor asked.

The second one nodded, "There was a weapons drop last night. We've been told to stop and search every vehicle to see if it's carrying weapons."

"Well, you won't have to worry about us! We're only carrying a shipment of vegetables," chuckled Cor, with a sinking feeling in the pit of his stomach.

The man handed back the papers, but he was more intelligent and less gullible than his partner. "We'll see," he said evasively. "Open the doors."

Cor was really getting worried now. Willem gently nudged him in the ribs and pointed to the accelerator with the tip of his shoe. Willem sensed that the smarter policeman would undoubtedly find the weapons and uncover their secret.

Their only chance was to make a quick getaway. But the gun was still aimed at Cor's head. They would have to do something to distract the men's attention.

Cor made as if to get out to open the back door. Suddenly, his eyes bulged as he stared out across the field.

"Look at that! I've never seen a hare that big!" His finger was pointing at a spot in the field behind the men. Both men, incurable hunters, wheeled simultaneously. "Where?"

"Behind that big bush!" replied Cor. Just then he rammed the accelerator down to the floor, and the van bolted off. The four men in the back went sprawling. Some of the wooden crates tipped over, spilling out potatoes and weapons. The van bounced and rattled off down the road.

There were two shots, and a rain of buckshots clattered against the armoured car. "Well done!" chuckled Willem. "The look on your face when you saw that hare was something else. I almost believed it myself!"

Cor grinned. "Hunting hares is all they're good for. They're too stupid to know anything about people," he sneered.

"Maybe we haven't heard the last of it yet," said Willem. He was clearly concerned. "We just passed a few houses and a coffee shop. There is probably a telephone there. I'm sure they'll send out an alert right away. They may have taken the licence number, but in any case they'll be able to describe the van. We're going to have to do something."

They turned off at the first sideroad, which took them out of their way. Continuing on the highway was far too dangerous.

They halted at an isolated clearing in the woods. They threw a tarp over the van, and Cor quickly replaced the licence plates. Fortunately, they always came prepared for emergencies like this.

The mess in the back was straightened out. "Well, let's try again," said Willem. "Listen guys, we're going to make a detour through the woods that will take us into the city from the other side."

It was a good thing that Cor knew where he was going. They picked their way along narrow, winding country roads and through a number of small hamlets. Willem kept his eyes open for anything unusual. Twice they had just enough time to take a sideroad when they spotted a roadblock further on down.

This trip seemed to go on forever. The men in the back of the bouncing van found their seating facilities less than comfortable.

Still, they made good headway; they had gone completely around the city and were approaching it from the other side. Cor and Willem, both exhausted from tension and the worry about what they should do if they were stopped, at last concluded that the worst was over.

But they had it wrong. Though getting close to the city, they were still driving through winding, wooded terrain. Every once in a while the road dipped sharply, making it difficult to see what lay ahead.

"Hey, Germans!" Willem suddenly blurted. And sure enough, down at the bottom of one of the dips in the road was a squad of Wehrmacht soldiers whom they hadn't seen earlier because of the hills.

There was no way out, and they could no longer turn around. They were trapped—or at least so it seemed.

Cor had an idea; at first he rejected it as unworkable and idiotic, but with no time to think of anything better, he decided he had to try it.

He rolled down his window, turned off the ignition, and put the gearshift in neutral. The van quickly gathered speed as it barrelled down the hill toward the men manning the roadblock.

The leader of the squad raised his right hand, ordering them to stop, and a number of rifles were turned on the van.

Cor stuck his head out of the window and yelled at the top of his voice, *"Kann nicht halten! Habe die Bremse kaputt!"*[17]

The bewildered German soldiers jumped aside, and the leader of the group didn't know exactly what to do. The van rumbled and quickly disappeared from sight around a curve. Cor then started the engine, put the transmission in gear, and shoved the accelerator down to the floor.

As he wiped the back of his hand across his brow, he noticed that his face was wet with sweat.

---

[17] Can't stop! Brakes are gone!

Five minutes later they were in the suburbs where three men were dropped off. Cor, Willem, and Blankers continued on to the warehouse.

They weren't safe yet. They might be stopped by the Germans patrolling the city streets. But nothing of the sort happened. They arrived at the old warehouse without further incident. Shortly after they had honked the signal, the large metal door swung open. They drove inside the courtyard and shut the door behind them.

"Well, we made it!" sighed Willem with obvious relief. Can't tell you how I felt though, when I spotted those Germans! The way you got us through that, Cor, was unbelievable!"

He laughed and slapped Cor on the shoulder.

Though Blankers hadn't seen a thing of what had happened at the roadblock, he was very happy that it was all over. When he spotted the friendly faces of Oom Koos and Tante Miep, he felt relaxed and right at home. He dearly loved the company of this elderly couple who had been so good to him.

They quickly unloaded the van, hiding all the weapons in a few gigantic wine kegs. Part of the cache was for Willem's operation. The rest would be stored until it could be picked up by other Resistance units.

Willem and Cor left, taking the empty van with them. Blankers accompanied the elderly couple to their apartment. After having a bite to eat, he went to bed to catch up on sleep he had lost the night before.

During the next few days he spent a lot of time on target practice. He'd been given a revolver equipped with a silencer. He set up a target in one of the wine cellars and practised diligently, determined he wouldn't be caught unprepared again.

He didn't actually like the idea that he might have to use his weapon to take someone's life, but he couldn't forget the feeling of uselessness he had had while riding in the back of the van. If it had come to a showdown, he wouldn't have been able to defend himself. That was incentive enough for him to keep practising. Each day he went back to it until he felt at home with the weapon.

Blankers was kept busy all the time now, mostly in the secret print shop. Every once in a while, Willem would show up with other members of the local Resistance unit. Willem had been trained as a weapons instructor, and now his task was to pass on his information to others.

They quickly learned all about guns and grenades and the like, but the most important part of the lessons concerned the use of sabotage materials such as explosives.

Among the explosives that had been dropped was the plastic kind that wouldn't explode even in direct contact with fire. It needed a special detonator cap to make it explode. The men were taught the tricky business of installing the caps. They learned all about fuses and time mechanisms, about how to install the explosives to get the maximum desired effect, and hundreds of other things.

Willem was a good instructor who insisted that his directions be followed rigorously. Even the smallest slip-up, he warned them, could have very serious consequences.

Explosives could come to play an important role when the Allies renewed their efforts at liberating the Netherlands. The men of the Resistance, now under the command of Prince Bernhard, would have to operate behind enemy lines to disrupt German defenses and help bring victory.

When would that time come? No one was more anxious for it than Blankers himself. Gradually they all began to realize that it would not happen this winter. The Germans had cut the dyke on the south side of the Rhine River so that a large part of the countryside beyond was flooded. Any military action south of the Rhine toward Arnhem was practically impossible.

Those days in December were very dark indeed; in the western provinces, millions suffered hunger. All along the front the Germans were digging in. No, the war wasn't over yet, and still heavier trials were sure to come.

To find out about these trials, and the victory which would follow, one can read the fifth and last book in this series: *SABOTAGE*.